SISTER ROSE'S SAINTLY SUSPECTS

Elder Wilhelm Lundel has a vision of returning the Shakers to their days of strength and glory, and there are those who would stand in his way.

Sister Elsa Pike is a rough, hill-country woman with spiritual aspirations and a shady past. Rose is her chief rival for the position of eldress.

Seth Pike, Elsa's son, had ridden the rails with the victim, but something split them apart. Seth is a bitter man with some secrets in his past—one of which involves Rose.

Albert Preston, a Shaker novitiate with his own secret past, claims not to have known the victim, yet they were seen arguing.

Sister Charity McDonald is young, pretty, and seems unduly anxious since the murder.

Molly Ferguson has many things a Shaker girl shouldn't have—lipstick, perfume, face powder . . . and a secret that could shed some light on the murder.

Other Avon Books by
Deborah Woodworth

A DEADLY SHAKER SPRING
A SIMPLE SHAKER MURDER
SINS OF A SHAKER SUMMER

DEATH OF A WINTER SHAKER

DEBORAH WOODWORTH

AVON BOOKS
An Imprint of HarperCollins*Publishers*

This is a work of fiction. Names, characters, places, and incidents either are the product of the author's imagination or are used fictitiously. Any resemblance to actual events, locales, organizations, or persons, living or dead, is entirely coincidental.

AVON BOOKS
An Imprint of HarperCollins*Publishers*
10 East 53rd Street
New York, New York 10022-5299

Published by arrangement with the author
Library of Congress Catalog Card Number: 96-97083
ISBN: 0-380-79201-X
www.avonbooks.com

First Avon Books Printing: April 1997

Printed in the U.S.A.

WCD 10 9 8 7 6 5 4

In memory of my mother,
Virginia R. Woodworth,
who taught me to love a mystery

ACKNOWLEDGMENTS

As I worked on this book, many people offered me support, encouragement, and, when necessary, delicately worded criticism. I want especially to thank my writers' group: George Sorenson, Tom Rucker, Mary Logue, Andrew Hinderlie, Peter Hautman, Charles Buckman-Ellis, Marilyn Bos, and Becky Bohan. My thanks, as well, to Mary Trone for her invaluable editorial advice; to my editor, Tom Colgan; and to agent extraordinaire, Barbara Gislason. And to my family, the Woodworths; Marilyn Throne; the Schiferls; and my husband, Norm—thank you for believing in me.

AUTHOR'S NOTE

The North Homage Shaker village, the town and the county of Languor, Kentucky, and all their inhabitants are figments of the author's imagination. The characters live only in this book and represent no one, living or dead. By 1936, the period in which this story is told, no Shaker villages remained in Kentucky or anywhere else outside the northeastern United States. Today one small Shaker community survives, Sabbathday Lake, near Poland Springs, Maine.

Deborah Woodworth
1996

PROLOGUE

A WOMAN IN THE LONG, LOOSE DRESS OF THE SHAKER sister twirled on the dew-soaked grass, her arms flung straight out from her sides. Her voluminous skirts billowed around her like a dark bell. She spun silently for a minute, then, still circling, raised her face to the sky. Her cheeks glowed with the first pink rays of sunrise.

The woman stopped and stiffened. Her body jerked as if racked by powerful spasms. Her heavy bonnet shook loose and tumbled to the ground. Within seconds, her legs collapsed beneath her. She crumpled and lay motionless, an enraptured smile on her upturned face.

Hidden in a thicket of sugar maples, a young man crouched in the dark, watching. A dry leaf tapped his shoulder as it fell toward the ground. He gasped and steadied himself against the rough, cool bark. He told himself it was the damp, autumn air making him shiver, not fear. He hadn't gotten where he was by being afraid.

As the silent figure peered into the gloomy clearing, the woman opened her eyes to the sky. She rolled to a sitting position, shook the dew from her bonnet, and retied it under her chin. She heaved herself off the ground and wiped her hands dry on her skirt. With a deep breath, she began to spin again. Words tumbled from her mouth, but not words her listener had ever heard. He'd ridden the rails with all sorts of folks, had heard German and French and even some Gaelic, and this was like none of them and all of them together.

Her watcher drew back into the darkness. Excitement made him careless, and he cracked a twig. Stifling a curse, he turned slowly and peered back into the clearing. The woman still twirled, heedless of any noise but her own strange language. The young man slipped away, smiling to himself. What he had seen could fit right into his plans, he thought. He nearly whistled but stopped himself just in time. He did not notice the third pair of eyes, watching him from the darkness.

ONE

YOUNG GENNIE MALONE'S LONG, DARK BLUE SHAKER cloak flapped behind her in the brisk wind as she wove through the kitchen garden on her way to the Herb House. Gennie could never resist a garden. During the summer, she had taken this path every day, no matter where she was assigned to work. She would brush her dress against the sweet lavender or chew on a sprig of spearmint when she thought no one was watching. By this time of year, the kitchen sisters had picked and preserved most of the vegetables and herbs, so Gennie had little to sniff or taste.

Glancing around her, the girl paused to lift the edge of her bonnet and pull a few locks of auburn hair free to curl around her face. Then she ran the last few steps through the wet morning grass to reach the Herb House. Sister Rose would follow her soon and expect her to be elbow-deep in dried caraway and dill seeds. Rose might overlook a few strands of hair in ringlets, but she would not tolerate sloth.

The white, clapboard building stood well back from the unpaved path that cut through the Shaker village. Half-hidden behind the Laundry and surrounded on two sides by herb fields, the Herb House felt like a secret hideaway to Gennie. She swept aside her skirt and eased open the door, always left unlocked. A warm cloud of strongly scented air enveloped her as she climbed the well-swept stairway to the second-floor drying room.

She paused halfway up the stairs to play her favorite guessing game. Inhaling deeply, she could recognize some of the fragrances, even this late in the drying process. She could distinguish pungent rosemary from the sweet rose petals, sage from lemon balm, all mellowed by the smell of earth and hay. That morning the air was especially sweet, almost sickly sweet by the time she reached the second-floor landing. Though it had not rained during the past week, the humidity must have been high enough to cause some decay.

Gennie stepped inside the drying room, her favorite place in the whole village. She'd live in here if Sister Rose would let her. Thick bunches of herbs hung upside down in rows from every possible peg, hook, and wooden drying rack. Long screens spread across tables held the smaller and more delicate items such as rose petals and thyme. The herb crops had been so full this year that the Society's carpenter, Brother Albert, had hung long hooks from the rafters to dry the excess. Closing her eyes, she flung out her arms and twirled around, enjoying the faint crackle and the release of fragrances as her fingers tapped a few nearby bundles of herbs.

When she opened her eyes, Gennie saw one loose bunch of catnip on the floor a few yards from her. She felt a prick of guilt, but quickly realized it was too far for her to have knocked the herbs from their high hook. As the stems dried and shrank, they sometimes slipped from the string used to bind them in bunches.

She'd better move the catnip to a safe place. Scooping it up, she ducked under a row of long tarragon stalks and found a drying screen covered with daisylike chamomile flowers. There was just room for the catnip.

Rose would be along soon, time to get to work. Gennie unhooked a bundle of feathery dillweed and made for the large worktable under the east window.

The table was long and solidly built. The sisters often sat around it to crumble and package seeds and dried herbs. On warm days, they would open the window, and she could hear them singing as they worked. The rising sun splashed light across the length of the table, across round metal tins waiting to be filled with dill-weed and lavender buds.

And across the still form of a young man. Gennie stared at his two bare, pigeon-toed feet. The dillweed crumbled in her clenched fists and trickled to the floor.

Slowly, she stepped closer to the still form. The cloying, moldy smell she had noticed earlier grew stronger as she neared him. She didn't want to breathe, but her pounding heart forced her to gulp the fetid air. She yanked a fresh handkerchief from her pocket and held it to her nose and mouth.

She clutched at the hope that the man might only be ill or injured. She might still be able to help him; she had to go to him, check for injuries. She forced herself to approach the man's face. His skin was grayish, his curly blond hair matted and dirty. Clearly, no one could help him now.

Gennie knew him. He was Johann Fredericks, a handsome and charming drifter who had arrived in North Homage about two weeks earlier. Gennie and her roommate, Molly, had noticed him right away at mealtime, eating silently across the dining room with the brethren. He had been quite a treat to look at. Of course, Shaker girls were not supposed to do any such thing. But they had, and giggled about it together later that evening in their retiring room.

Now Johann, though not a Believer, wore the plain, dark work clothes of the Shaker brethren. His trousers were too short for his long legs, revealing several inches of dirty ankle. Dirt clung to every visible part of his body. His bare toes looked as if they had been dredged through the mud. Gennie stared, horrified, at his grimy hands. They were crossed over his chest in a gesture of final peace. Beneath the hands lay a bouquet of dried herbs and flowers, tied with a frayed bit of twine.

Gennie backed away and stumbled from the room.

TWO

THE WORRIED EXPRESSION ON SISTER ROSE CALLAhan's pale, lightly freckled face softened for a moment as she gazed out her office window and saw Gennie skim around the limestone corner of the Trustees' Office.

Gennie was her favorite of the young girls being reared by the North Homage Shakers. Rose hoped she would choose to sign the covenant and join the Society of Believers when she reached eighteen in a few months. Bright, young Believers were all too rare these days. But Rose remembered what it was like to be seventeen, though it was nearly half her life ago. She remembered how it felt to be lured by the bright, false promises of the world.

Rose turned back to her desk, shaking her head at the memory of her own youth. A few tendrils of curly red hair pulled loose from her white cotton cap. She pushed them back under the fabric with a practiced movement and reached for the cup of rose hip and lemon balm tea she'd brewed for herself in the small Trustees' Office kitchen. The tea had grown cold, like the air in her office, but it brought comfort. Like work and song and prayer, the daily taste of the tea, sweet and rich, bound her to the Shaker life.

She had no regrets, she told herself. The call to become a Believer, the call that had brought her back to the Shakers seventeen years earlier, was as clear and strong as ever. All the stronger, she believed, because she had known worldly love before choosing to devote her life to the Society.

Some of the other sisters believed that any venture into the world was dangerous. But Rose disagreed. If a young woman belonged in the world, she should be there. If she then chose the Society over the world, knowing what she was giving up, she'd follow the teachings of their foundress, Mother Ann, through eternity. But Rose knew only too well how few young people chose the Society over families of their own. She had watched North Homage's alarming decline for many years.

Rose sighed and pulled her work toward her. Copying numbers into a ledger book for the second day in a row had brought her aching shoulders. To ease them, she pressed back against her firm ladder-back chair, crafted by Brother Hugo especially to fit her tall, thin body.

As the only remaining trustee of the North Homage United Society of Believers, now known even to themselves as Shakers, Rose was responsible for the community's financial well-being, as well as relations between Believers and the outside world. Now thirty-five, she had been a trustee for ten years, and they had been good ones. Perhaps her humility needed further development, but she felt she had been born for this position.

She examined her figures with satisfaction. Even in these dark times, the small squares on the ledger page added up to a comfortable total. Demand had been steady for packaged seeds and preserves and other Shaker products. Most of their northern Kentucky neighbors had not fared so well. Rose was pleased they were in a position to donate a goodly amount of produce to the poor.

"Gazing into space to rest from thy exhausting

labors?" Elder Wilhelm Lundel's voice dripped with disdain. At sixty, the spiritual leader was an imposing, muscular man with a full head of white hair. His broad shoulders nearly touched the sides of her office doorway. He wore the brown smock and slate gray trousers of the nineteenth-century brethren. As required in the Society's earlier days, he was clean-shaven. The stern set of his jaw made clear his displeasure with Rose. Again.

As part of his plan to create a Shaker rebirth, Wilhelm had adopted the old-fashioned form of Shaker speech, using the more formal "thee," rather than "you." Rose allowed herself the uncharitable thought that he had done so in part because it made his words sound weightier.

"If this calling is too difficult for thee," Wilhelm continued, "I'm certain we can find others eager to replace thee."

Rose clenched her teeth in irritation. Eldress Agatha had taught her a prayer when she was a quick-tempered child—*Mother Ann, lend me thy patience and humility.* She used it often with Wilhelm. Rose raced silently through the prayer four times before her jaw began to relax.

Calmer, she met the elder's eyes. "You should take a look at these numbers, Wilhelm." She slid the account book off the desk and held it out to him. "We're doing well."

"Financially, perhaps. For now." Wilhelm did not even glance at the page. He lifted a ladder-back chair from a wall peg and sat facing Rose, more than half a room between them. "Spiritually," he said, "we are rotting away."

Rose relaxed her tired shoulders against the slats of her chair back. "I'm well aware that we are growing smaller," she said, with the weary air of one who has endured the same argument many times too often.

"Smaller! Hah! We are near death. A hundred years

ago we had more than four thousand Believers. Four thousand! And now the eastern societies have fewer than one hundred among them.

"We are all that is left of the western societies. Pleasant Hill, South Union, the Ohio and Indiana societies, they are all nothing but empty, rotting buildings. And why?" Wilhelm leveled a thick index finger at Rose. "Because they turned their hearts to the world, that's why."

"The world is changing," Rose objected. "Our strength has always come from our ability to adapt and give to the world. We do well in troubled times because we invent tools which save effort. We share our inventions with the world and gain friends and Believers. Brother Hugo came to us at first because we gave him a chance to develop his carpentry skills most creatively. And he has been a devout Believer for nearly sixty years now!"

"They wallowed in luxury and adorned their bodies shamelessly," Wilhelm continued as if she had not spoken. "They spurned the simple life of worship and hard work and modest dress, and they pandered themselves to the world. They were lost to God. And that is the result of thy 'adapting to the world.'" His sneering tone made her words sound foolish and shallow.

Rose sighed. What was truly foolish, she knew, was to continue the argument.

"What brings you here, Wilhelm?" Normally he would have summoned her to the Ministry House, to show who was elder and who was merely trustee.

"Eldress Agatha."

Rose snapped to attention. "Is she all right?"

Her mentor's failing health worried Rose for many reasons beyond the loss of her friendship. Until a year ago, when she suffered her first stroke, Agatha had been more than a match for Wilhelm, but now Rose found that the task of tempering Wilhelm's religious fervor fell to her. As Agatha sank, Wilhelm soared. At his insistence, North Homage Believers had reverted to nineteenth-century Shaker dress.

"She is too ill to continue," Wilhelm said, his heavy face showing no sorrow. "I am recommending to the Lead Society in Mount Lebanon that Agatha be relieved of her duties as eldress."

He can't even wait for her to die, Rose thought. Agatha's body might be weakening, but the two strokes had barely touched her mind. Rose felt her quick temper rising. Aware that Wilhelm was watching her reaction, she tried to give him none.

"And who will you recommend to become the next eldress?"

"Not thee." Wilhelm leaned forward and planted his fists on his knees. "Thy past shows a certain . . ." His eyes glittered as he sought the most cutting words. "A certain spiritual weakness."

Rose bit the inside of her lip. Her past again. Her year in the world. She had returned at nineteen, confessed at worship service to the whole community, and been welcomed home. Wilhelm was the only one who continued to use her past against her. She tried to pray, but this time anger won.

"My past is long past, you know that well, Wilhelm. I've confessed, I've atoned. Now it is up to God alone to judge me."

"As I've no doubt He will." A small smile played on Wilhelm's wind-roughened lips. "Meanwhile, I have another plan for thee. One which may help thy redemption."

Rose's fury dissolved into wariness. "What might that be?"

"I have a journey for thee to undertake, beginning in March, when the weather warms. I want thee to lead the conversion of souls throughout Kentucky and Ohio."

"Wilhelm, that would be a mistake. We aren't in the

eighteenth century anymore. These are the 1930s, the country is tired and hungry. It has no energy for revivalism. We should help people now, not stir them up. As long as God feels we have work to do, He will provide us with the help we need."

Wilhelm stood and gripped the back of his chair, his eyes blazing. "We have a sacred calling, given to us by our beloved Mother Ann. We are called to save as many poor wretches as possible from their disgusting, carnal lives in the world. What good does mere charity do them? What is a full belly compared to the eternal joy of life as a Believer?"

Rose wilted in her chair. So this was his plan to dispose of his two most outspoken critics. By March, if Wilhelm had his way, not only might she lose her position as trustee, she would be sent away from her home on a mission she couldn't support. And dear, wise Agatha would no longer be eldress.

Unless the Lead Society in New York interfered, Wilhelm would hold total control over North Homage. And he would drive them straight back to the eighteenth century. Her head had begun to throb, a common result of any discussion with Wilhelm.

Startled by a sudden movement, Wilhelm and Rose turned to the open doorway. Gennie leaned against the doorjamb, her small chest heaving with the effort to catch her breath, brown eyes wide with terror.

"Oh Rose!" she whispered. "It's so horrible."

THREE

EVEN WITH THE GREAT DEPRESSION IN FULL SWING and hobos wandering from town to town, violent crime was rare in small, rural Languor County, Kentucky. The Shakers' reputation for generosity brought many hungry, homeless men—and sometimes women and children—to their door. But not everyone admired the Believers. Some resented them for their stores of meat and vegetables, and the shiny, black Plymouth parked next to the Trustees' Office. Their refusal to fight in war, even to defend their country, infuriated many. So the discovery of a murdered man in North Homage's Herb House stirred both anger and glee in many of their neighbors' hearts.

"We haven't had a murder round here in five years," the county sheriff, Harry Brock, said when he arrived at the Trustees' Office steps at midmorning. "Funny it happened here, ain't it?"

Sheriff Brock's thin, wiry form seemed to shift constantly. His suspicious eyes darted between Wilhelm and Rose, who stood a respectable distance apart. Running a distracted hand through his thick white hair, Wilhelm fastened his fierce eyes on the horizon. A still-shaken Gennie huddled beside Rose. The sky was splotched with black, and a growing wind whipped at Rose's cloak. She drew the thick wool closer.

"Sheriff Brock," Rose said, raising her voice to

command his attention. "We Shakers do not murder. To kill another human being goes against our most sacred beliefs. It is abhorrent and certainly not funny."

To her discomfort, Brock grinned at her. "Yeah," he drawled, "but here we are. Funny."

Curious Believers had begun to cluster nearby. A plump, middle-aged sister, Elsa Pike, elbowed through a group of whispering women. She ignored Rose and barged toward Wilhelm. Elsa's behavior no longer surprised Rose, but she had grown increasingly concerned that Elsa seemed to respect only Wilhelm.

"Elder, we gotta do something," Elsa said, anger pinching her plain, flat features. "Word's out that we killed somebody. That's hogwash, pure and simple, everybody knows we Shakers don't kill, but there's horses and wagons comin' in already, just to see for themselves. Couple folks even stopped at the kitchen and asked the way to the body, of all the nerve. And if they think I'm going to cook for them and make it a party, well, they got another—"

"Elsa!" Wilhelm rarely used a sharp tone with Elsa. It silenced her. "Yea, a young man has died, but of course we did not cause it. Go back to thy work now. There will be no extra cooking. The gawkers will have nothing to feed their disgusting curiosity."

Elsa hesitated. "This young man, was he one of us? One of the brethren?"

"Nay, only a Winter Shaker, and not a promising one."

"I knew it," Elsa crowed. "It's that Johann, ain't it? He was askin' to get killed, the way he carried on. And with sisters and young girls, too." Her smirk was more self-righteous than shocked.

"Hush," Wilhelm urged. He glanced at the sheriff, who had hurried off toward a tall young man just emerging from a dusty black Buick used by the Languor County Sheriff's Office. Wilhelm almost pushed Elsa away, but stopped himself before he actually touched her. "Be careful about statements like that if the police question thee. Now get back to the kitchen."

Looking pleased with herself, Elsa trotted away on strong, hill-country legs.

Molly Ferguson, Gennie's roommate, stood apart from the crowd. She balanced a laundry basket on one hip, and her dark eyes fixed on Gennie. With a flick of her index finger, Molly signaled for Gennie to approach her. Molly's eyes were wide and murky, her cheeks paled to a ghostly white against the black rim of hair edging her bonnet.

Behind her, a group of men, mostly brethren, milled at the base of the Trustees' Office steps. Elder Wilhelm murmured with Brothers Albert and Hugo and a tall, weathered man Gennie did not recognize. His head tilted toward Wilhelm, but he watched Rose. Rose's attention was on Brock. She wouldn't miss Gennie for a moment or two.

"Hurry," Molly whispered. She clutched Gennie's wrist in a painful grip. "The sisters in the Laundry said you found a dead guy."

Gennie winced and nodded.

Molly's eyes went black. "Shaker?" she asked.

"Nay, don't worry," Gennie said.

"Who was he? Did you know him?"

"Yea, but just by sight."

"Gennie," Rose called, "we need you now."

"What was his name? Tell me," Molly whispered, her husky voice straining with urgency.

"Johann Fredericks." Gennie tossed the name over her shoulder as she raced back toward Rose. When she arrived, breathless, she turned to wave to Molly. The laundry basket lay overturned, clean work smocks cascading onto the grass. Molly's running figure receded toward the fields behind the Children's Dwelling House.

* * *

"This is Deputy Grady O'Neal," the sheriff said, indicating a tall man in his mid-twenties with straight brown hair that fell forward whenever he moved. "Did you get hold of Doc Irwin? Good. This here's Gennie Malone, the young lady who found the body."

Everyone turned to look at Gennie, who straightened at being called a young lady.

"We'll need her statement," Brock continued.

"I'll stay with her while you question her, if you don't mind," Rose said. Her tone said that it didn't matter whether they minded.

"We'll look at the scene first," Brock said. "Here's Doc now."

"Gennie, you stay here," Rose said, placing a warm hand on her shoulder.

"Sorry," Brock said. "We'll need her to tell us what everything looked like when she entered the building, what she moved or touched."

"But she's only a child." Rose's arm went around Gennie's shoulders and held tight.

"Then she's a child who found a dead body," Brock said bluntly.

"Besides," said Deputy O'Neal in an educated voice that just covered a gentle Kentucky drawl, "she seems to be holdin' up fine." He smiled over at Gennie, who smiled back and shyly lowered her eyes.

"Let's go, then, but you stay close to me, Gennie." Rose cringed inwardly as she noticed the glance that passed between Gennie and the young deputy. She would have to talk with Gennie soon.

The Herb House door swung open easily and released the jumble of odors that Gennie had so welcomed earlier. But now the too-sweet smell was dominant, or perhaps she was more aware of it, knowing it signaled human decay. Rose scooted quickly through the door, holding her cloak so that it would not touch Deputy O'Neal, as he stood aside for them to pass.

"My guess is the deceased's been dead for a while," said Doc Irwin, Languor's only physician, as they entered the second-floor drying room. He didn't elaborate.

Returning nausea made Gennie's stomach churn, but she clenched her teeth to control it as Doc Irwin approached the table where Johann was laid out. He leaned over and peered at Johann's head and neck. He lifted aside the filthy hands, unbuttoned the shirt, and examined the chest area, then replaced the hands in their funereal pose. Gennie saw Johann's chest for just a moment before Doc Irwin moved in front of him.

"Stab wound," he said quietly.

Sheriff Brock leaned his head toward Grady. "Looks like that fella won't be bothering Miss Emily anymore, don't it?"

As he stared at Johann's body, a flash of anger distorted the deputy's boyish features. In a moment, his expression cleared. He turned to Gennie.

"Miss Malone—is it Sister Gennie?" he asked.

"Just Gennie."

"OK, just Gennie, are you up to answering some questions?" He took a small notebook and a pencil stub from his coat pocket.

"Of course," she said, with what she hoped was spirit.

Grady regarded her speculatively. "When you arrived this morning," he asked, "did you touch anything in this room?"

"Yea, I picked up a bunch of catnip that had slipped from the string holding it together." She neglected to mention her high-spirited twirling among the hanging bunches.

"Did you notice any signs of a struggle?"

"Nay." Gennie recounted for him as best she could her passage through the room toward Johann, as Grady scribbled in a small notebook. Then it came time to look once more at Johann's body. Rose held

Gennie's hand as they walked to the table. The others stood aside to let her have a clear view.

"Miss Malone," said the sheriff, "all Doc did was he just opened the deceased's shirt and lifted up his hands and put them down again the same way. So think hard. Did you touch him or move him or anything?"

Gennie forced herself to look at the gray remains of Johann Fredericks. His Shaker work jacket had fallen open. Through the fingers of his right hand, she could see no rip in his shirt, no sign of a stab wound. She'd seen one before on the leg of a hobo who had come to the Trustees' Office door for help. The man's pant leg had been drenched with blood, and that was only from a small leg wound. But no blood stained Johann's white smock and jacket.

Gennie wondered why she hadn't noticed before such a clean smock on a filthy Johann. Then the truth struck her. The herb bouquet on Johann's chest had so riveted her that she hadn't seen the state of his clothing. She noticed now, though, because the bouquet was gone.

"Well?" Brock prodded. "That how you found him?"

"Nay, that isn't how I found him," she said, slowly shaking her head. "Someone moved the bouquet."

"What the—what bouquet, what are you talking about?"

"When I found him, there was a bouquet of dried herbs and flowers in his hands. It was so strange . . . almost like he'd been dressed for a funeral." Gennie saw puzzlement and disbelief in the faces of her listeners, all but Brock, whose foxlike features grew thoughtful.

"You mean one of those bouquets hanging here?" he asked, jerking his head toward a small sheaf of lavender hooked on a nearby drying rack.

"Nay, it was more like a real bouquet, with different

flowers, but this one was dried." Though Shakers never used flowers for adornment, Gennie remembered the enormous clusters of daisies and zinnias her own mother had loved to scatter around the house.

"Gennie, this has been a shock for you," Rose said. "It may have seemed as though you saw a bouquet just because you were surrounded by flowers and—"

"Nay, I *did* see a bouquet," Gennie cried. She appealed to Grady. "You believe me, don't you?"

Grady smiled sympathetically but said nothing. Sheriff Brock, however, grinned in a way that unnerved Gennie.

"If she did see what she says," he said, "it'd be mighty interesting, wouldn't it? Makes me wonder real hard what somebody around here was up to."

Wilhelm had commandeered the Trustees' Office, situated at the entrance to North Homage, from which to fend off the curious and none-too-friendly townspeople who had begun to collect. Rose worried that Wilhelm might incite the crowd, not calm it, but she couldn't be everywhere at once. She led Brock, Grady, and Gennie from the Herb House, past partially cleared herb fields, across the village's unpaved, main path, and up the walk to the Meetinghouse.

The most important building in the village, the Meetinghouse was painted, repaired, and scrubbed with care. A picket fence with two gates surrounded the imposing, white structure. One gate opened to a pathway and the east door, to be entered only by men, and the second led to the west entrance, reserved for women. Most buildings in the village contained separate doors and stairways for men and women, to prevent their brushing against one another.

Out of habit, Rose pushed open the west gate. She should have sent Brock and Grady through the east door, but she was too tired to force the issue. If

Wilhelm saw them follow her through the women's entrance, he would use it as yet another example of her unfitness to lead. She hurried them inside.

A large room, a full two stories high, occupied much of the ground floor. Sunlight streamed through deep-set windows taller than a man. A doorway at the east end opened to offices and to a narrow stairway, which climbed to a second-floor observation room. From a small window in this room, the Ministry—the elders and eldresses—kept an eye on Believers and outside guests during a worship service. If anyone were up in the darkened room now, Rose thought, they could watch the interrogation without being observed. She hoped that the gathering crowd would keep Wilhelm busy. The less involved he was in this investigation, the more relieved she would be.

Rose and Gennie lifted two straight, ladder-back chairs with woven seats from the pegs that lined the walls and placed them side by side on the spotless pine floor. Grady grabbed two more and put them much too close to theirs. Rose moved the chairs farther apart. Gennie started to sit across from Grady, but Rose gave her a firm push to the next chair.

"Miss Malone," Brock began, as Grady pulled out his pad and licked the tip of his pencil, "anything else you want to tell us? Like, how well did you know this Johann Fredericks?"

"I hardly knew him at all," she replied. She bit her lip but her voice was steady. "How could I? He was a man, and only a Winter Shaker anyway. I know who he was, that's all."

"Whadd'ya mean, a Winter Shaker?" Sheriff Brock said sharply. "Why'd you call him that?"

"Some people come to us in autumn, professing a wish to become Believers," Rose explained, "but all they really want is food and clothing and a warm place to live for the winter. They leave us in the spring. So we call them Winter Shakers. We try to give to the world as best we can, but some people take selfishly." She could have added that they planted more sweet corn and potatoes than they needed, so their neighbors could raid Shaker fields when their own larders were empty. But she doubted Brock would be impressed.

"You got a lot of folks like that?" Brock asked.

"Quite a few," Rose answered. "These are difficult times. This depression has thrown many people into the streets. We can hardly turn them away."

Brock's calculating eyes shifted to Gennie. "So, Miss Malone, do you know all the Winter Shakers?"

Gennie shook her head.

"Any reason you'd know this one?"

Rose lightly touched Gennie's arm, and said, "Tell him what you saw, Gennie."

Two male heads popped to attention.

"What? What did you see?" Brock directed the questions to Rose.

Rose folded her hands together again. "You should hear it first from Gennie. She'll have seen much more than I could, since I was talking to Brother Hugo about bookbinding and carpentry. As I'm sure you understand, my attention was divided." A smile teased the corners of her thin lips.

"All right, then," Brock said, leaning back in his chair. "What'd you see, Miss Malone?"

Gennie hesitated.

"It's all right," Rose said, smiling at her. "I saw you watching them, and I followed your gaze. I know you did not tell the monitors, but then neither did I. What's done is done. Just tell what you saw."

Gennie gazed around the vast, sun-speckled room. "It happened here. You see, we are having Union Meetings again," she explained, "once a week, because Elder Wilhelm thinks we should go back to the old ways."

Brock looked blank and shifted impatiently.

Rose leaned forward. "The meetings are so the

sisters and brethren can chat together," she explained. "They are a kind of controlled social gathering. Elder Wilhelm feels that our behavior has been too loose in recent years. At times, sisters and brethren have laughed and talked together right in the street. Now we must save our conversations for the Thursday-night Union Meeting. We have monitors who keep an eye on them and guard against special looks between men and women."

Brock and Grady exchanged horrified glances.

"Real interesting," Brock said. "But what's it got to do with this murder?"

"Last Thursday," Gennie began, "I was sitting with the children, watching the talking."

Rose thought back to the meeting. The sisters had sat in one straight row, hands folded right over left. Now and then a hand was raised to gesture, then carefully refolded. Several feet across from the sisters sat the brethren, their chairs spaced more widely so that one man could talk to two women, since there were twice as many women as men in North Homage.

"There really wasn't much for me to do," Gennie continued, "so I . . . I made up a game. I tried to guess what everyone was talking about just from how they looked, you know, their faces. I watched Charity—Sister Charity McDonald—for a while, and—"

"Why her?" Brock demanded.

Gennie looked flustered.

"We both noticed her," Rose said. "She looked troubled." Charity was no more than twenty-three and very pretty, in a wispy way. With the whites showing all around the green iris, her eyes seemed forever startled, but Thursday evening she had seemed especially edgy.

"All right, so what'd you see?" Brock snapped.

"Charity and Johann . . . they looked at each other," Gennie said.

"They looked at each other," Brock repeated.

Gennie nodded. "Johann was standing with the other guests, and Charity looked right over at him."

Rose, too, had seen the special look, though Gennie had been closer. She remembered Johann leaning against the doorjamb, his shiny blond curls curving out from under his woolen cap. He had smiled crookedly in Charity's direction and bowed his head slightly.

Brock was silent for a few moments. Grady O'Neal sat with his pencil poised.

"And?" Brock asked finally, an impatient edge to his voice.

Gennie looked up at him in surprise. "Well, that's all I saw. You asked what I saw. They gave each other a special look, and Charity blushed."

The sheriff snorted and rolled his eyes toward the ceiling.

"Kid," he said, "I don't care how special it was, if looks could kill, we'd have a prison on every block. A look don't mean nothing in the eyes of the law." He sprang up from his chair and paced.

"Now, you sayin' those two was having a fling or something? You got hard evidence, like maybe you seen them fooling around behind the barn?"

"Sheriff!" Rose bolted up, ramrod-straight. At five-foot-eight, she could look Brock directly in the eye. "You know perfectly well that if any of us had found that Charity and Johann had fallen prey to the flesh, they would have been sent away instantly."

Brock stopped pacing and faced Rose, a grin slowly forming. "Yeah, I know that. Just wanted to see what the girl would say." He turned to Gennie. "Well, girl? Seen anything like that?"

"Nay," Gennie said forcefully, "I saw no such thing."

Brock shook his head and leaned toward Grady, but his words were swallowed by loud bursts of noise, piercing the normally quiet village air every few seconds. Grady bolted up so quickly that his chair clattered backwards. Both men rushed through the door and toward the road, kicking up billows of dust. Rose and Gennie followed quickly.

A small crowd had gathered at the foot of the steps leading to the Trustees' Office entrance. Elder Wilhelm, planted on the top step with his arms outstretched, shouted to the air above the townspeople. His stern features hardened with the fierce concentration Rose had seen during his worship service homilies. Sister Elsa's plump figure stood two steps below him.

"Come and join us," Wilhelm shouted. "Live a pure life. Give up the sins of thy wretched flesh, which make thee no better than the beasts in thy barns . . ."

Sister Elsa nodded over and over, her eyes closed and her face toward the sky in trancelike agreement.

Renewed blasts blotted out the rest of Wilhelm's exhortation. Now Rose identified the source of the racket. The sheriff's office's two Buicks were parked by the Trustees' Office, next to the Believers' shiny, 1936 Plymouth. In Languor County, no one locked doors of any kind, except maybe to the liquor cabinet, if one were lucky enough to have such an item. So the three sets of car doors swung wide open, and all the cars were stuffed with as many men as would fit inside. Those in the front seats jabbed incessantly at the horns.

"What the hell!" the sheriff shouted as he and Grady bolted toward their own cars. They grabbed arms and legs and dragged squirming bodies through the open doors. They pulled out at least ten laughing young men before turning their attention to the crowd, which shouted and clambered up the steps toward Wilhelm and Elsa. Rose noted that the sheriff did not bother to rescue the Society's Plymouth.

The townspeople were only a few steps from Elsa

and the elder and showed no signs of stopping. Their taunts grew louder and angrier. Wilhelm stood firm, one arm raised to the heavens as if calling down the thunder. Elsa had begun to fidget, her eyes darting between the approaching crowd and her leader. She eased backward up a step to be closer to him.

Grady raced up the steps two at a time, followed more leisurely by Sheriff Brock. Grady elbowed his way through the crowd. A muscular young man in the streaked dungarees of a farmhand knocked Wilhelm's flat-crowned straw hat off his head just as Grady reached the front of the crowd. Grady clamped his hand over the young man's wrist.

"No, Tom. Don't do anything we'll both regret."

"Grady, you heard him same as me. He was blaspheming!" Tom tried to wrench free of Grady's grasp.

"Now, you two, that's enough," Brock said as he rounded the edge of the group. "Tom, cool down now. Maybe he's blaspheming, but . . ." Brock half smiled and shrugged his shoulders. "The law says he has a right to. You and me, we may not like it. But you hit him, and I gotta arrest you, and I'd hate to do that, Tom."

Tom glanced uncertainly at Brock and back at Grady, then dropped his arm.

"All right, ya'll head home now," Brock said to the silenced townspeople. "You let us take care of things here. I promise you, we'll do just that."

Rose was grateful to see the crowd disperse, though the sheriff's parting words gave her more than a twinge of uneasiness. Her previous dealings with the world had been conducted with mutual respect, even when she'd driven a hard bargain to purchase land. It worried her that such hostility had simmered so near the surface.

She sought out Josie, an older sister and also the Infirmary nurse, watching from a safe distance. Josie was no supporter of Wilhelm and made her opinions known, with the courage of the elderly, as often as she wished.

"What can Wilhelm possibly have been thinking?" Rose asked.

"What a moment to begin converting new Believers to the faith," Josie said with a quick, mirthless laugh. She shook her head, jiggling several chins in the process. "I'm glad I'm too old to be picked for Wilhelm's revival mission. I fear this is the reception they will find."

FOUR

ROSE COULDN'T FACE AN AFTERNOON OF FINANCIAL accounts, not after the morning she'd just endured. She needed outdoor work. She assigned herself to pulling onions, since they were short of hands to complete the harvesting. Everyone, including the ministry, was expected to participate in the endless physical tasks necessary to keep a Shaker community fed and clothed. The founders had hoped that work would humble leaders who might think themselves better than the ordinary Believer. The idea appealed to Rose, but she doubted whether it really worked, remembering Wilhelm's arrogance a few hours earlier.

Before she rounded the back corner of the Herb House, where the neglected onion bed lay, Rose heard two furious male voices.

"You've got no right to treat me like dirt," said one angry voice. "I'm as good as you, every bit."

"You were trying to get inside, weren't you? Maybe the police would be interested in that. Maybe I should just call them now, eh?"

Rose recognized the second voice as belonging to Brother Albert Preston, the Society's carpenter. She'd never heard him speak above a low, shy rumble before.

Hearing sounds of a scuffle, Rose rushed the last few yards around the building. Albert faced her, grimacing as he fought off the second man's grip on his upper arms. Short and gaunt, Albert was no match for the taller, more muscular man. When he saw Rose, he paled and stopped struggling. His assailant spun around.

Rose gasped. Hard years had etched craggy lines in his face, but the old intensity still burned in his hazel eyes. It was Seth, Seth Pike. She hadn't seen him for seventeen years, and she'd thought, hoped, that she would never see him again. Foolish, of course. He was Sister Elsa Pike's son. Naturally he would return.

He smiled and tilted his head at her. "Hello, Rose," he said. "I'm back."

Seth spread his arms, and for a moment Rose thought he would hug her. She stepped back involuntarily. Seth dropped his arms. Rose glanced at Albert and saw speculation in his eyes.

"What's been going on here," she asked quickly. "Brother Albert?"

Albert wasn't really one of the brethren yet, just a novitiate, but the Society accorded him the title out of desperate need for new male Believers. He was normally reserved and took little part in the worship services, especially the dancing. A remarkably skilled and hardworking carpenter, Albert was the only hope for their furniture business, now that Hugo, nearly ninety and growing blind, was unable to work.

"Caught him trying to sneak into the Herb House," Albert said. "Police said no one was to go in until they'd had more of a look around, so I came over to put a lock on the door. Good thing I did."

"I was just walking past, OK? You were the one trying to sneak in, far as I could see." He poked his index finger into Albert's chest and pushed him a step backward. "I've got as much right here as anybody else. Mr. Lundel hired me to work, and that's what I'm doing."

"What's to work on around here?" Albert challenged him.

"These onions, for one," Seth said. "They've been ready for weeks, by the look of them."

"I don't believe you—"

"All right, both of you, that's enough," Rose said sharply. "I want you both to go back to your work, whatever it was, as long as it isn't here and preferably at opposite ends of the village." She ought to question Seth, but she didn't trust herself yet.

With a last glare at each other, they stalked off. Before disappearing around the Herb House, though, Seth paused and turned back to Rose.

"Glad to see me, Rosie?" He turned again and was gone. Hearing one of his old nicknames for her startled her, but she was relieved that none of the old feelings stirred. Seventeen years was a long time. Maybe she would visit Eldress Agatha. The onions could wait.

"I trust Gennie is recovering from her terrible experience?" Eldress Agatha Vandenberg rocked herself gently. She was small-boned and thin. A worn blue quilt covered her lap and spread over the arms of her wooden rocking chair. To Rose she looked more fragile every day, her skin like rose petals left too long to dry. On her lap lay an open book containing the sayings of Mother Ann.

"Gennie is resilient," Rose assured her.

Agatha nodded once. Her faded blue eyes focused inward on eighty-five years of memories. Her hand absently stroked a thin, satin ribbon sewn into the book's binding as a marker.

The only other chair in the eldress's sparse room was a three-slatted wooden one near the desk. Rose moved it close to Agatha and waited patiently, knowing that the eldress would break the silence when she was ready.

"Will she stay, do you think?"

"Gennie? I don't know. I hope so."

"You must work hard with her. She would make a good Shaker. A good Shaker."

Agatha focused her filmy eyes on Rose. "You are troubled. Do you have an idea who might be responsible for that poor young man's death?"

"Nay, it's nothing so important." Rose took a deep breath. Her own concerns seemed petty compared with Johann's death, but Agatha was her confessor. "Seth Pike is back."

"Ah."

"Wilhelm has hired him to work here."

"And this is difficult for you? Do you feel tempted?" Agatha's soft voice had an edge of sternness.

"Nay, truly I do not. He does not even appear to be the gentle man I once knew. He is bitter, combative." Rose shook her head. "I have made mistakes, and I regret them still."

Agatha smiled. "Rose, my dear, remember that our Mother Ann married and bore children. Her understanding came later and after the loss of all those children. We are all weaker than Mother Ann, of course. We can only aspire to her strength and purity of spirit. To believe that you should never make mistakes—well, that is hubris. And to hang on to your regret long after you have confessed and been forgiven, that, too, is false pride." Her eyes twinkled through the cloudiness that signaled advancing blindness. "Besides, there are plenty of fresher sins to worry about."

Rose laughed, and her pale face brightened. As always, Agatha's wisdom had brought her "round right." She sobered quickly as Agatha sank back in her chair and lowered her chin as if slipping into sleep.

Rose frowned. How could Agatha, weak as she was, straighten out any of this mess? Rose knew, from stories told by older Believers, just how violent their enemies had become in the past. During the previous century, it had been common, especially during hard times, for North Homage's neighbors to set fire to the Shakers' buildings. Such violence was part of the past Wilhelm yearned to recreate.

Agatha's eyes shot open. She sighed and closed her book on the satin bookmark. "So many are leaving, so many of the young and strong."

"We have always lost many youngsters to the world, but others have come to take their place," Rose said, as much to convince herself as to comfort Agatha. "Sometimes they leave and come back, as we both know."

Agatha gave her a rare and gentle smile. "You see, you learned well from your time in the world," she said. "It will help to make you a better eldress, when I am gone."

"Agatha, don't. All you need is rest and—"

The eldress waved her hand impatiently. "When you are eldress," she continued, "you must not allow Wilhelm to force his will on the Society. His will is strong. It would almost be better if I could go soon. You are so much stronger now than I am."

"Agatha—"

"Nay, listen to me. You are right when you say that new Believers have always come. But they will stop coming if we continue down Wilhelm's path, farther and farther into the past. Our strength lies in our faith and our purity of living, not in costumes and behaviors that seem strange in the world's eyes. New Believers will come only if they respect us and want to be like us." Agatha smoothed her hand over the soft blanket. "Then again, maybe we have done our work and it is time for all of us to let go."

Rose remained quiet. At thirty-five, she was far too young to consider her work done and the Society's mission accomplished. But she was unsure whether she was the right choice to lead them forward. She thought of herself as a practical, day-to-day sort of person. Her spiritual understanding needed much deepening. She preferred not to face the issue yet. Agatha would get well; she had to.

"Enough of that," Agatha said. "I do hope Gennie stays with us. There is evil waiting for her in the outside world. And now it has reached into our midst."

Rose touched Agatha's thin shoulder. "The police will find the person responsible for the killing, surely."

"Perhaps, perhaps." The eldress spoke softly. Rose leaned close to hear and smelled the fragrance of lavender that clung to the quilt.

"We have been touched by evil before," Rose said firmly, "but never consumed by it. Remember that Mother Ann was attacked by an angry mob, but she endured it all, and the Society only became stronger."

Agatha seemed to return from far away. "I remember that speech," she said, raising her pale eyebrows at Rose. "As I recall I gave it to a certain young Rose Callahan, who had been teased by some village children and thought that she would be seen as weak if she didn't break their little noses."

Rose laughed with delight. "Well, then," she said, "it is tried-and-true."

With a swift movement, the eldress clutched Rose's hand in a surprisingly tight grip. "You must seek the truth, Rose. The police do not know our ways. They cannot understand. You can. You know us, and you know the world. You know what to watch and listen for. I am very afraid that the misguided soul may be one of our own."

"Are you saying that a Believer may have killed Johann Fredericks?" Until that moment, Rose had not taken seriously the idea that a Shaker, having taken a vow of nonviolence, might be responsible for the murder. Nor had she realized the danger the Society would be in if this proved to be the case.

"Oh, I don't know, I don't know," the eldress said.

"Perhaps. And perhaps the police will think so." She released Rose's hand and held her book against her chest as if it were a restless infant. "I only know that I grow weaker, and I cannot do what must be done. But you can, Rose, and you must."

"Truly, I don't see what I can do. I've no training in police work, no experience—"

"Rose," Agatha interrupted sharply, "your humility is admirable, but not what is called for here."

"I'll do what I can," Rose said quietly. To be truthful, she knew she would not have been able to leave their fate in the hands of the police. She rose from her chair and moved it back to its place at the desk. "Will you rest now?"

"Yea, yea, don't fuss over me." Agatha's old spirit came and went now. Sometimes she was her strong, old self, impatient and demanding of perfection. At other times, she seemed fragile and frightened.

Rose bent to kiss the soft white hair, free of the gauze cap that the eldress normally wore even in private. As Rose reached the door, Agatha said softly, "There are secrets in our community, Rose. More than you know. Find the truth."

An hour of yanking onions, perhaps harder than they needed to be yanked, lightened Rose's gloom. She allowed herself to begin thinking about what Agatha had asked her to do. Distasteful as the idea was to her, she knew she was the best person to tackle the search for Johann's killer. As trustee, she was the only one used to working with the world, and she knew everyone in North Homage. Sheriff Brock longed for the killer to be a Believer. He wouldn't look farther than their gate.

Rose slapped an onion against the hard ground to free its roots of dirt. A few loose clumps stuck to the skirt of her long, loose outdoor gown, and she quickly brushed them off. The dark blue wool hid most stains, but the dress wasn't due for washing until later in the week.

As she tossed the onion into her basket, she glanced up and saw that she had company. Unwelcome company. Elder Wilhelm stood at the end of the row, his burly body straight, legs apart and arms stiff at his sides.

"Agatha is not well," he said. "She was not thinking clearly when she asked thee to meddle in this affair."

"Agatha's body may be weakening, but her mind is as quick as yours or mine," Rose said firmly. "If she wants me to investigate this tragedy, I most certainly will." She yanked up a large onion and held it in front of her like a shield—and a reminder to Wilhelm that she had work to do.

Wilhelm's right hand clenched. Rose saw his fist and questioned, not for the first time, the power of Wilhelm's loyalty to his vow of nonviolence.

"I should not have to tell thee what it means to be a Believer," he said, his rich voice sharpened by irritation. "But apparently we have expected too much of thee. This eagerness to meddle in the world, these defiant words . . . a clear lack of humility. This is not the behavior of a leader. I should relieve thee now of thy duties."

His words dropped like sharp knives at Rose's feet, and she twitched as though they had struck her.

"You haven't the authority to do so," Rose said in a voice turned cold and hard as Kentucky limestone. "Not alone. I believe that Agatha is right. Because of my experience and my position, I am the one who must find Johann's killer. No matter who it is."

Wilhelm paced between two rows of brown, shriveled onion stalks, his hands clasped together behind his long, dark coat. As he turned again to Rose, his hard blue eyes glittered with cold anger, and his mouth formed a thin slash across his face. Rose stood her ground.

"Agatha and I disagree on many things," Wilhelm said. "Her mind has grown old. I reason with her as best I can, and she has often come to see that I am right. She cannot live much longer. And when she is called back to God, I will have much to say about who will take her place. She will not be here to protect thee."

"Agatha is my friend, not my protector," Rose said. "You are mistaken if you think that I expect to become the next eldress."

"Good," Wilhelm said, crossing his arms over his thick chest, "because I have decided who is to be the next eldress."

Rose did not ask who that might be, only tilted her head as though politely interested.

"One of our newer members has the right qualifications, I believe," Wilhelm continued, with a firm nod of his head. "I've been impressed with the devotion she has shown by leaving her husband and sons to join us. She will bring enthusiasm and new spiritual energy to the Society. Through her gifts, we will again draw in hundreds."

"Can you mean Elsa Pike?" Rose couldn't keep the astonishment out of her voice.

"I can and I do."

"But Elsa can't possibly be ready for such a responsibility. She's so new and so . . . unschooled in our ways." What Rose meant was that Elsa was unschooled altogether. She had lived in North Homage for about a year now, only six months as a full-fledged sister. She had not gone through the Society's excellent school system, nor any school system beyond the third grade. *No doubt she's a good woman,* Rose thought, *but an odd choice for eldress.*

"Her gifts are natural; she does not need further

education," Wilhelm said, a defensive edge to his voice.

"What does Agatha say about—?"

"Agatha will not be here when the decision is made, will she?" Wilhelm smiled, a rare occurrence, and usually not a pleasant one. This smile was no exception. "Elsa has gifts we have not seen the like of for a hundred years. It is Mother Ann's Work once again; Mother Ann is working through Elsa, and she means to make us strong again. Already, Elsa has given us two spirit drawings and a dozen new dances. And there will be much more that will surprise thee. Soon, very soon."

Elder Wilhelm tipped his hat to Rose, then looked down a row of onions. "Thy harvesting is not finished," he said. "Hands to work." With that, he disappeared around the corner of the Herb House.

A part of Rose wanted to believe that Wilhelm might be right about Elsa and the gifts she seemed to display. From the 1830s to the 1850s, the Society had experienced a tremendous revival, which they called Mother Ann's Work. Believers fell into trances and spoke with lovely angels, who filled them with powerful words and sweet songs. Some Believers received, in visions or in their dreams, gifts of intricate drawings or prophecies or messages from long-dead Believers. Others spoke unknown languages. Outsiders flocked to the worship services, and many new converts signed the covenant. It was an exciting time, but it ended badly, as Rose recalled. Eventually, the derision of the world had forced the Society to close its worship service to the public.

Wilhelm was a powerful man, in many ways. The Lead Society—Mount Lebanon in New York—would surely listen to him if he recommended Elsa for eldress. Rose wasn't certain that she wanted to be eldress herself, yet she disliked the thought of Elsa taking the place of her much-loved friend, Agatha.

During her novitiate period, Elsa had had plenty of opportunity to learn about the gifts. Was she clever enough to use her knowledge to impress Wilhelm? *Who am I to judge,* Rose thought, *whether her gifts are real?* Yet she trusted neither Wilhelm nor Elsa.

FIVE

"I'D RATHER HARVEST THE PUMPKINS."

"Yea, Gennie, I know. But you're needed in the kitchen, and that's that." When Rose said "that's that," it was. She sounded unusually brusque now, too, so it wouldn't be wise to argue.

"You've had a trying day, you needn't begin instantly," Rose said, more gently. "Do as you please for an hour, then report to Charity in the kitchen." She flashed Gennie a tired smile and left her alone.

Free time was rare in North Homage. Gennie sought the farthest herb fields, with spiky thyme plants awaiting their final harvesting. She paced the rows. Out of habit, she brushed her cloak against the branches to release their spicy fragrance. But for once it gave her no pleasure. Her mind was elsewhere.

Gennie was not enjoying her freedom. Shock had set in and, along with it, other feelings that she had more trouble identifying. New feelings, ones that she couldn't share with Rose.

A twig cracked behind her. She whirled around to see Grady O'Neal coming toward her, his hands in his jacket pockets, shoulders hunched against the wind.

"Hi, there," Grady said. "The sheriff's taken off, and I was having a last look around outside the Herb House. I saw you head out here all by yourself. Still upset, are you?"

"Nay, I . . . well, a little, but . . ." Gennie took a deep breath. Her hands were trembling, so she thrust them under her cloak.

"Did you have more questions for me?" *There,* she thought, *that's much better, much steadier.*

Grady smiled broadly and shook his head. Brown hair fell over his eyes. "Nope, just thought I'd come over and see how you're doing. Talk a spell, maybe."

"We shouldn't, you know."

Grady looked puzzled. "Yeah, I got that idea from Sister Rose telling us about Union Meetings, but I thought that with me not being a Shaker and all . . ."

"It's not that," Gennie explained. "It's that you're a man. I shouldn't talk to men alone, at least not for long. Don't you know about us? Didn't you grow up around here?"

"Yup, Languor-born and -bred," Grady said. "Left for a couple years of college in Ohio, but otherwise I've been here all my life. I love it here, came back as soon as I could."

Gennie nervously scanned the area around the Herb House. She saw no one. With a twinge of guilt, she made a decision.

"Let's walk farther out," she said. "There's a crick behind those trees. I wander there sometimes, when I can get away."

Grady grinned and approached her.

"Nay," she said quickly. "Stand away a bit."

They walked in silence, several yards apart, stepping carefully over the rows of short thyme plants. They entered a clump of oak trees with leaves just turning a golden brown. Gennie's excitement gained strength over her guilt.

"You sit there, on that rock," she ordered. She smoothed her cloak under her and arranged herself as gracefully as she could on the grassy stream bank. She wanted to skip a stone across the water, but she was afraid that it might look childish.

Grady obediently parked himself on a large, flat rock, which overlooked the water.

"You're fond of Sister Rose, aren't you?" he asked.

"Of course. She's been as good to me as my own mother."

"Will you stay with her?"

"Become a sister, do you mean? I don't know. I suppose I'll have to decide soon. I'll be eighteen in a few months." Sometimes Gennie was mistaken for younger because of her size, and she wanted Grady to know that she was nearly grown.

"What does being eighteen have to do with it?" Grady inched across the rock, closer to her, and leaned forward.

"Eighteen is the first time I'll be asked if I wish to become a Believer," Gennie explained. "They'll ask if I want to sign the covenant."

"What's that?"

Gennie's smooth forehead furrowed in concentration. "It's a promise. If I sign, I promise to follow the Shaker ways. I wouldn't be just myself anymore, I'd be a small part of the Society, and everything I own would be everybody's. My work would be for the whole village and not for me alone. They'd be my family, and I'd have to promise not to have any other." She lowered her eyes shyly.

"Will they kick you out if you say 'no'?"

Gennie laughed. "Nay, of course not. Rose would probably let me stay forever, but it wouldn't be fair of me. I'd hardly be any better than a Winter Shaker then, would I?"

Grady eased forward again and dangled his long legs over the rock's edge.

"I doubt that you have to worry about that," he said. "When the time comes, I bet you'll make the best decision."

Gennie played with a blade of grass. "Thank you,"

she said faintly, feeling as if this meeting surely wasn't her best decision. Yet it felt good. Very good.

Grady slid his legs back on to his perch and sat cross-legged, his elbows on his knees.

"So," he said, settling his chin on his hands, "tell me what is so wrong about me being a man and you being a woman."

Gennie gulped. "It's not that there's anything wrong with that really, it's just . . ."

"Yes?"

Gennie was foggy about the Believers' theological reasons for remaining celibate. To be truthful, she and Rose had never discussed the topic. The sisters who had taught her in the Shaker school until she turned fourteen had been vague. They'd used terms like "carnal relations," which sounded intriguing but meant little to Gennie and the other girls.

"Well, you know, Jesus never married," she said in a halting voice. "So the Shakers believe that's just the most blessed way to be. Not married."

"Then how do Shakers make babies?"

Gennie grabbed a small stone and flung it across the water, where it skipped once before sinking into ripples. Normally she could skip up to five times, but her hand was shaking. She was in over her head.

"A lot of us are orphans," she said, rather than answer Grady's question directly. "The Shakers took us in and raised us. My father brought me to live here just before he died in 1929."

"I'm sorry," Grady said. "Did he . . . did it have anything to do with the stock market crash?"

"I don't know," Gennie said. "I wish I did. I miss him. And my mama, too."

Grady leaned over and picked up a smooth stone. He rubbed his fingers over it as though judging its skipping potential. He took careful aim and flipped it toward the water, where it skidded six times.

"I want you to know, Gennie Malone, 'just Gennie,'" he said quietly, "that I'll respect your ways. But at this moment I wish I could take your hand."

Gennie reported for kitchen duty feeling a guilty glow that faded quickly as she endured the feuding of the two kitchen sisters, Charity McDonald and Elsa Pike.

"It were a judgment, I reckon," Sister Elsa pronounced. A plump and muscular countrywoman with the plain, flat features of a local native, she pounded rather than kneaded the large lump of bread dough in front of her. She had taken over the breadmaking without asking permission from Charity, who was kitchen deaconess. It was a battle that Charity had chosen not to fight, but Gennie was disappointed. She liked making bread, especially when she could experiment with herb breads. She'd especially loved making "Rosemary's Muffins" from a recipe Rose had created when she wasn't much older than Gennie. But Elsa insisted that plain food was best, and she looked down her nose at the Shaker herb industry. Salt and pepper were spice enough for her, mostly salt.

"A judgment. Wouldn't you say, Sister?" Elsa directed a piercing look at Charity, who stood facing the sink, washing up the many pots and pans they had dirtied since lunch.

Charity increased the volume of hot water surging into the sink. She did not turn around. Under the pale gold hair that pulled free of her white gauze cap in soft wisps, a mottled redness crept up the fair skin on the back of her neck.

When Charity had finished the washing, she turned to the open hearth, where a large kettle of beef stew simmered in preparation for the evening meal. As she stirred, she stared toward the strip of wooden pegs along the wall, from which hung silky copper-bottomed pans, kitchen utensils, and even a broom.

She gave no sign that she was anything but alone in the room.

"What was that boy doing in the Herb House, anyways?" Elsa continued, when it became clear that Charity was ignoring her. "Meetin' someone, one of them girls from Languor, more 'n likely. Better not be one of ours." She looked hard at Gennie.

At this, Charity turned her startled-doe gaze toward Gennie. "Elsa," she said, still watching Gennie. "Remember it was Eugenie who found—let's drop the subject, shall we? For Eugenie's sake."

"Well, I just wonder what he was doing in the Herb House, that's all." Elsa gave the bread dough a swift punch with her broad fist.

"As far as I could tell," Gennie ventured, "Johann Fredericks wasn't doing anything in the Herb House except being dead. I don't think he was even killed there."

Elsa's eyes widened until they were almost the size of Charity's, and both women paled. Questions hovered on their lips. But neither said a word, either then or for most of the remaining afternoon.

Gennie was pleased with herself. If she'd tried with all her might, she couldn't have found a better way to still the bickering between the kitchen sisters. She didn't think deeply about the significance of her guess, nor did it occur to her to wonder about its meaning to Elsa or Charity.

SIX

For the Shakers, Wednesday and Thursday passed in building tension. A constant string of visitors trampled the grass around the silent Herb House, which the police had cordoned off and secured with a padlock. A few townspeople arrived in cars and dressed in their Sunday best, others by horse or on foot in their workaday dungarees. A reporter and photographer from the *Cincinnati Enquirer* set up their equipment in the middle of the herb garden to get the best shot of the building and to collect stirring interviews with shocked and curious bystanders. The sheriff visited regularly, but he did nothing to stem the flow of intruders. His only interest seemed to be in the Herb House, where he spent hours searching each day.

The Believers were too busy to talk to reporters or to worry much about the behavior of outsiders. This time of year, the harvest ruled their daily lives. Everyone except the ill and feeble arose at 4:30 A.M., had a quick breakfast, and hurried to their assigned tasks. During harvest season, they often settled for only one more meal, a hearty picnic out in the fields, so they could continue to work until darkness forced them to quit. Wilhelm canceled the Thursday night Union Meeting. There would be no break from the work.

Unless they had special skills, most Believers worked

in four-week rotations. A sister might spend four weeks in the kitchen, followed by a rotation in the Laundry, and then the sewing room. Despite their belief in the equality of the sexes, Shakers divided work according to gender, with women performing domestic tasks. It was far more important, they felt, to keep the sexes separate, and if they worked together, anything could happen. During the harvest, though, men and women often worked side by side.

As trustee, Rose oversaw work assignments, though theoretically her decisions were subject to approval by the Ministry, Wilhelm and Agatha. Agatha always supported her. If she was lucky, Wilhelm ignored her. Just now, all three agreed that every available hand should rescue the apple crop before it fell to the ground and rotted.

Rose had reluctantly assigned Gennie again to the kitchen to help with the apple pies and applesauce. She knew how much the girl disliked kitchen work. But she was the best worker among the young girls, and Charity always requested her.

On Friday morning, Rose decided that Gennie deserved a break and invited her along to the farmers' market in Languor. An ecstatic Gennie clambered onto the front seat of North Homage's sturdy black Plymouth. After a thorough cleaning and buffing, only a deep slice in the seat betrayed the car's rough treatment by young rowdies on the day of Johann's murder.

Under Rose's firm touch, the Plymouth spurted to life. Rose and Gennie remained silent as they began their eight-mile drive into Languor. For a time, they watched the rolling countryside and rich fields bounce by.

"You're so quiet, Gennie. I hope you aren't too frightened by all that's been happening. It will be over soon, I promise you. You won't have to be involved anymore. I'll arrange for you to have an extra rotation in the Herb House once the police give it back to us. Would you like that?"

Gennie twisted in her seat. "I'm not frightened," she protested, "not really."

Rose's mothering smile faded. "You've been through a lot for someone so young, and I feel that—"

"I'm almost eighteen!" Gennie bit her lip and sat back against her seat. "I'm sorry, Rose, I shouldn't have raised my voice." She stared out her window.

These flare-ups had become more common in recent months. Rose remembered herself at Gennie's age, and she worried. She flashed Gennie a quick smile.

"All is forgiven, Gennie. You are right, you're almost eighteen, and I'll try not to treat you like a child."

They reached the outskirts of the town of Languor, population 2,520, mostly poor. Rose slowed down to a crawl as they passed the crooked shacks that housed the poorest. As always, the big, black car drew attention from dirty, running children and jobless men sitting on broken stoops. One man raised a pint bottle in ironic greeting, since Shakers were known to be teetotalers, then lowered it to his lips. A woman hanging laundry glanced over her shoulder at the car, then shouted to a little girl sitting in the grass near the road. The child jumped up and ran to her.

The car headed for a group of older boys playing baseball in the road with stones and a stick. Rose had used the horn with the occasional cow, but never with people. Now she edged to the right as far as possible to avoid the boys without disturbing their game. Two boys moved aside to let the car pass. But another, apparently the pitcher because he held a large rock in his hand, whirled on the car and glared at its occupants.

"Rose?"

"We'll be through here in a moment, Gennie."

As the bulky Plymouth passed him, the boy pointed a ragged arm at its occupants, his fist wrapped around the rock. He shouted something Rose couldn't hear. Then he shouted again, louder, his thin face contorted with hatred. "Witches," he shrieked at them.

"Rose, he's following us!"

The small back window of the Plymouth exploded inward, spraying shards of glass across the spacious backseat. A rock, slowed by the impact, fell spent on the seat.

Startled, Rose swerved farther to the right and onto the grassy shoulder. The Plymouth stalled. Still within range of the boy, she could see his angry, triumphant face. She stepped on the starter button, shifted, and pressed hard on the accelerator, but the wheels spun deeply into the soft shoulder. She pulled on the brake, pushed Gennie's head down beneath the level of the dashboard, and leaned over her back to shield her. They waited, barely breathing, listening. A loose sliver of glass tinkled as it fell belatedly. The boy's shouting had stopped. They heard no children's laughter, no mother's call. In fact, they heard nothing at all.

Rose raised her head. She slowly lifted her upper body from Gennie's bent back but with one strong arm held Gennie's head down, out of sight.

"Stay down. I'll check outside." Rose reached for her door handle.

"Nay, you mustn't get out of the car!" Gennie grabbed at Rose's arm. "One of those boys threw that rock. He might hurt you. Please can't we drive on?"

But Rose had already turned the handle and cracked open her door. With her free hand, she squeezed Gennie's shoulder and gave her a smile that didn't cover the worry in her eyes.

"If he wanted to hit us again, he's had his chance. Anyway, I need a rug from the trunk to help us get the car unstuck. We'll have to make arrangements in

Languor for repairs." She stepped out of the car, sweeping her skirts behind her. For Gennie's sake she tried to appear fearless.

"Nothing to be frightened of, they've gone," she reported cheerfully, as Gennie rolled down her window. "Not a soul around. But you'd better stay inside, just in case." She reached over and patted the girl's arm, then straightened. She stood on dry and weedy grass which served as lawn for a ramshackle cottage. Three chairs, all empty, faced the road from the middle of the yard. The windows were shaded against the daylight with tattered brown curtains. One of the curtains twitched as if it had just been dropped into place.

Rose's unease grew with each moment outside the car. She hurried to the trunk and pulled out two rag rugs. She could hear the light tinkle of shattered glass as she closed the trunk lid. Bending quickly, she spread the rugs in front of the Plymouth's back tires.

With her heart thudding heavily, Rose took one last look around. Where the boys had played baseball, there was only an empty, dusty street. No children laughed and chased one another from house to house. The man with the whiskey bottle had disappeared. A basket still heaped with laundry sat on the ground next to a clothesline that held a white blanket neatly hung with clothespins for half its length. The other half grazed the dirt below.

Gennie scrambled out of the car to huddle beside Rose. The girl's shoulders were hunched in fear as she wrapped herself tightly in her cloak. Her eyes were wide and dark, like those of a wary cat.

"Don't you notice it, Rose?"

Rose's breath caught in her throat. She listened now to the silence. Circling slowly, she peered down the empty street and abandoned yards. She caught a sudden movement by the corner of a nearby house. Just a hint of sleeve, the flash of sun on a stone surface.

"Gennie, get in the car. Now!" The girl obeyed instantly.

Her heart lurching, Rose dragged open her own heavy door and jumped inside, barely pulling her skirts off the narrow running board in time to avoid catching them as she slammed the door. She hit the starter button. Through clenched teeth, she mumbled an urgent prayer of supplication.

As the Plymouth sputtered to life, another rock whipped through the shattered back window with force enough to slam the back of Gennie's seat and thud to the floor behind her. Gennie instinctively slipped down in her seat and pulled the hood of her cloak over her head.

"Good," Rose said. "Stay down, we'll be out of this neighborhood soon."

The car lurched and the tires skidded briefly, then slipped onto the rugs. At once the Plymouth shot back onto the road, spitting the rugs out from under it. Rose pushed the sturdy automobile to speeds it had not yet experienced in its short life. It bounced wildly over the ruts in the old dirt road.

They reached a quiet residential street, lined with elm trees that touched in graceful arches over the center of the road. Rose pulled the car over to one side, and folded a trembling Gennie into her arms. At that moment, Gennie had to be a child again.

In a few moments, the girl pushed away and sniffled. "I'm okay," she said as she pulled a handkerchief from the sleeve of her dress and swiped impatiently at her nose. Her lapse into childhood was over.

"Do you feel up to talking to the police?"

Gennie nodded bleakly. "Why did they do that to us?"

Rose sighed and leaned back against the black leather. "Because we Shakers are being blamed for Johann's death, and for other problems, as well. This has happened to us before, though you've never had to witness it. We are different. We dress oddly, we worship strangely, we create our families differently. We often have better crops and more food than our neighbors. So some people say that we must be evil, maybe we're able to cast spells or some such ignorant nonsense. If something goes wrong, it seems easy and convenient to blame the odd ones. The parents talk about it, and the children act." Rose glanced back at the shattered rear window.

Gennie sat up straight and pushed her handkerchief into the pocket of her cape. "My eighteenth birthday is coming up in February, you know."

Rose watched her in silence.

"Well, I don't know if I really want to be different," Gennie said, without meeting Rose's eyes. "I just don't know."

"Perhaps we could talk about it later, when all this has settled down?" Rose eased the car back onto the street. Gennie stared at her hands as they drove the two remaining blocks to the Languor County Courthouse, which housed the sheriff's office.

SEVEN

EVEN IN SUCH A POOR AREA, THE COUNTY COURT-house dominated the town center. A broad flight of stone steps, worn in the middle, led to story-high, wooden double doors, ornately carved with motifs of tobacco leaves. The building itself, of large limestone blocks, looked more impressive from a distance. Up close, the doors needed sanding and painting, and years of grime stained the limestone. Shaker buildings were simpler but far cleaner.

Rose and Gennie clattered across the large rotunda, over a huge map of Kentucky formed with colored stones and painted slate tiles. The gold outline of Languor County had nearly worn away. They climbed a scuffed marble staircase and pushed open a frosted glass door with COUNTY SHERIFF'S OFFICE painted in large, black letters. A broad, oak bar, once varnished but now dull and gouged with cigarette burns, stretched the length of the room, separating the sheriff's office from the public.

The officer on duty sprawled at a desk behind the wooden barrier. A hefty, broad-faced man, he made the cluttered desk look a size too small. A coffee-stained copy of the *Cincinnati Enquirer* shared the desktop with a cracked coffee cup and an ashtray spilling over with cigarette stubs.

"You're sure someone attacked your car, Miss Callahan?" the officer asked without leaving his chair. "But you didn't see who did it?"

"Because the rocks were thrown from behind, as we told you." Rose spoke each word with the weary patience of one who has said the same thing three times over.

"Yes'm," he said, with a longing glance toward the newspaper. "You think you were attacked by a young boy. Look, I can see how you two ladies might of been spooked by a rock flying up and hittin' the car." He glanced at Rose's thin shoulders and smirked. "Those roads are tough driving, even for a man."

"If you'd care to examine our car," Rose said, barely controlled anger seeping into her voice, "you'll find one rock is resting on the backseat and another on the floor. Believe me, they are far too large to have flown up, as you suggest, and hit the window on their own."

The officer remained seated, an inert lump.

"Perhaps we should just wait for Sheriff Brock or Deputy O'Neal to return," Rose said.

"I don't reckon they'll be back for hours. They're both out at the Pike farm, tryin' to calm down old man Pike and that younger son of his. Some feud goin' on with their neighbor, Peleg Webster. Say, don't Peleg's farm border on your land?" A local feud aroused more interest in the man than an alleged attack on Shakers, that was clear.

"The Pikes are saying that Peleg's hogs is gettin' into their corn. So they're doin' their own butchering." He laughed hoarsely at his own joke and ended on a cough. He pulled a pack of Camels out of his shirt pocket. After selecting one, he started to put the pack away. He paused, narrowed his eyes, and tapped the top to loosen one cigarette. With a lopsided grin, he leaned forward and held out the pack.

"Have a smoke?"

"Nay, but thank you," Rose said evenly. "We gave them up long ago."

Gennie beamed at Rose, delighted. But she wondered, too, why the officer wouldn't believe them and even tried to embarrass them. She had made many trips to town with Rose before. Sometimes children stared at their clothing or pointed and laughed, but an adult usually shushed them. No one had ever tried to hurt her. And this policeman, why wouldn't he help them? If only Grady were here. He would believe them.

"Perhaps you would be good enough to bring me some paper and a pen," Rose said, "and I'll write a note for Sheriff Brock or Deputy O'Neal."

Sighing loudly, the officer shuffled papers in search of a blank sheet. As he did so, a young woman glided into the office. She closed the door behind her and stood framed against the frosted glass, as though waiting for all eyes to turn toward her. North Homage still nurtured a small silkworm industry, so Gennie recognized the fluid softness of fine silk in the bright red dress that clung to her slender form. Smooth blond hair capped her heart-shaped face. Red lipstick, brilliant against her fair skin, matched her dress. The scent of roses drifted behind as she pushed forward with her hips and swayed across the room.

"Hiya, Miss Emily," the officer said, his face lighting at the sight of her. "Grady said you was stopping by. He said to wait in his office."

Emily bestowed a closed-mouth smile on the group, lingering on Gennie's plain, dark clothing and bonnet. Without a word, she swung her hips toward a closed door behind the reception desk.

They all watched her slide through the door, the officer visibly savoring every movement. Gennie felt a pain that was new to her, like a cramping of the heart. Grady's girlfriend. That had to be who she was; she looked like a girlfriend. She hadn't worn a ring, so maybe she wasn't his wife, not yet anyway. Emily was the name the sheriff had mentioned as they'd examined Johann's body, and Grady had looked so angry. Had Johann tried to take Emily away from him?

Soft hair and swaying hips and a red silk dress, not yards and yards of dark blue wool and a stiff bonnet. Gennie glanced at Rose, who was handing her completed note to the inattentive officer. Had Rose ever wanted to float in red silk? Her eyes wandered back to the closed door of Grady's office and back to Rose. The trustee was watching her intently, her head tilted to one side and a worried furrow between her brows.

"Come along, then," Rose said firmly, "we've done all we can here, and it's growing late. We've some tasks to do in town before evening meal. There is no time now to have the car's window fixed. I'll ask one of the brethren to arrange for its repair."

A few moments later they descended the worn stone steps of the courthouse. Two blocks brought them to Languor's open-air marketplace, which showed the Depression's effects on the rural town. A café and rows of old shops, some slanting and all badly in need of paint, lined three boundaries of a dirty, cobblestoned square, converted each Friday to a farmers' market. The western border of the square opened onto a park, or what would be a park if it were cared for. Benches, spotted with bird droppings, scattered in no particular pattern on the crushed, brown grass. Near the park's center stood a large kiosk, still showing patches of bright blue paint, where the small Languor band had played bravely through the 1929 stock market crash and the first few years of the Depression. Now the instruments were silent, sold long ago for spare parts to repair farm machinery bought on credit.

Rose and Gennie wove through the open town square, among stalls filled with produce. Each stall had its own special scent, from sweet-tart apple to the grassy smell of fresh corn. The horse-drawn farm wagons added the familiar odors of manure and damp earth.

"Do we really need potatoes?" Gennie asked as Rose picked through a pile of them in one of the first stalls they came to.

"We'll need extra, I'm afraid. We'll probably be feeding the whole town on Sunday. Hold this for me, would you?" Gennie draped the solid, well-worn basket over one arm. She watched as Rose examined each potato, feeling for soft spots, before placing it in the basket. So many questions spun in Gennie's mind. Her feelings seemed to tumble over one another, creating the force of a midwestern tornado. Intent on her task, Rose's movements were so quick and sure, her features composed. She seemed completely recovered from the frightening attack on their car and the unsympathetic reaction of the police officer. But Gennie remembered Rose's response when the officer had mockingly offered her a cigarette, and it made her more approachable.

"Rose," she said, "I was wondering about something you said back at the sheriff's office." Her voice came out in a nervous squeak, and she fumbled with the nearly full basket.

"What would that be, Gennie?"

"What you said about smoking. That you've given it up, I mean. You didn't really, did you?"

"When have you ever seen me smoke, now, I ask you?" Rose grinned as she selected one last potato and placed it carefully in the basket.

"Never. But, I mean, you didn't really smoke, did you?"

"Many Believers did, you know." She raised her eyebrows at Gennie. "I hope you will not take that as permission to smoke. Most of us gave it up many years ago, when we decided that it might not be healthy, though we delayed much longer than the eastern Believers."

Gennie was still puzzled and showed it.

"All right," Rose continued, "I'll explain. Believers used to smoke pipes mostly, sisters and brethren both, but it's been, oh, nearly one hundred years since we stopped. Once, early last century, I've heard that Believers in several villages expected Mother Ann to appear to them, and they actually held a smoking meeting to honor her arrival. Brethren and sisters both smoked for an hour in a closed room." Rose snickered. "I don't suppose any of them cared if they ever smoked again after that!"

All the stories Gennie had heard before painted the old Believers as saints, or nearly so. Gennie felt more comfortable knowing that maybe they were human, too, and she was pleased that Rose had shared the story with her.

"We angered our neighbors when we stopped, of course," Rose continued in a more sober tone. "Many of them were and still are tobacco farmers. That young deputy, Grady O'Neal, his family became quite well-to-do tobacco farming. That is how he was able to attend college." Gennie felt her cheeks grow warm at the mention of Grady's name.

Rose touched her lightly on the shoulder. "Gennie, we'll have a talk, you and I, very soon. You are growing up so quickly."

Before Gennie could respond, she heard a familiar voice. Rose heard it, too, and they both turned to see Grady himself gesturing angrily to a man several stalls away. The man was half a head taller than Grady, with muscular shoulders squeezed into a tight flannel work shirt. Gennie felt there was something familiar about his broad face, distorted though it was in anger. She turned to ask Rose about him and was surprised to see her frown.

"Who is that, Rose? Do you know him?"

As if he had heard the question, the man looked over at them, his eyes barely brushing Gennie and locking on Rose.

Rose raised her chin a fraction and took Gennie by the elbow. "Come along, I'll introduce you. You may as well meet him, and we need to speak with Grady, anyway. I have some questions for them both."

The men watched as they approached. Gennie wanted to swing her hips, just a little bit, even though her efforts would be hidden by her heavy clothing. She glanced just beyond Grady to a park bench where a blond vision in red silk, now warmed by a rabbit's fur jacket, sipped Coca-Cola from a bottle with a straw. She sat on a spread-out newspaper to protect her expensive dress. Her silk stockings glowed in the sunlight.

EIGHT

ACUTELY AWARE OF THE FARMERS AND TOWNSPEOPLE crowding near the potato stall, Rose led Gennie as close as she felt she could to Grady and the man he'd just been arguing with. "Gennie Malone, meet Seth Pike," Rose said, meeting Seth's eyes only briefly.

"Mr. Pike," Gennie asked, "are you perhaps kin to Sister Elsa Pike?" The penetrating gaze shifted toward her.

Rose fidgeted with the button on her cloak. Grady's observant eyes darted from Rose to Seth and landed with a small smile on Gennie.

"Sister Elsa," Seth said with a snort. "Yeah, that's me. The sister's son." His eyes slid to Rose. "Her first little mistake. Eh, Rose?" He picked up a crate and balanced it on the edge of his stall. Swiftly, he began to fill the crate with unsold potatoes, his muscular arms straining against the flannel shirt as he reached across the stall.

"Rose," Grady said, "your note said that your car was hit by a rock?"

Rose noticed his reluctance to say that they had been attacked. She also noted that Seth paused with his back to them, as if listening.

"A boy threw the rock," Gennie said. "I saw him. At least . . ." She hesitated. "I did see him through the window as we passed him, right up close. And I saw his arm go up. But I didn't see anything else. And then, after we got out of the car because we were stuck, there was no one around. No one at all! They were all hiding, of course. We knew something was wrong, so we tried to leave, but the car got stuck. Then the second rock came. It had to be thrown by someone, it just had to be. We were so frightened."

"That's a rough neighborhood out there," Grady said. "Anybody with a car can attract attention from that sort. If someone did throw a rock at you, it was probably just envy that you all have a car and plenty of food on the table. I wouldn't worry too much about it. But I'd go home the long way, if I were you." He reached out to pat Gennie's arm reassuringly, then pulled back quickly.

"Nay, you must listen to us. The attack was against us, as Shakers, I'm certain of it, and Rose thinks so, too. The boy looked hatefully at us, and he shouted something, I don't know, something like 'witches' and 'devils.' He wanted to hurt us!"

Rose took Gennie's hand and held it tightly.

"Let's not make too much of that sort of talk," Grady said, a shade too heartily. "We've all lived and worked side by side now for many years. Surely, no one hates you Shakers any longer. Those days are long gone."

"Ha!" Seth Pike's voice pierced the air. He lifted the crate he was filling and dropped it with a thud on the display shelf of his stall, smashing potatoes underneath. "Be careful who you talk for, Grady O'Neal. Some of us don't have much use for Shakers. They steal away our families and our sweethearts and twist 'em up inside."

"Seth, for goodness sake, your mother wasn't rejecting you when she joined us," Rose snapped. "She made her own choice, just as I made mine. We heard a call you did not, and that's all there is to it. It's no one's fault."

Seth's eyes bored into Rose as a mocking smile spread across his face. "Maybe not such a good choice if one of you is a murderer. Oh, yes, I know all about Johann, so does everyone. We were friends, more or less. Did you know that? We rode the rails together, him and me, all last year, 'til I got word about this feud of my pa's. Johann rode on back here with me."

"I'm sorry, Seth, I didn't know."

"Yeah." Seth flung a potato into the crate.

"Where was Johann from, do you know?" Rose asked.

"California," Seth said, wiping his hands on his overalls. "Rode the rails all the way to Minnesota, but it's gettin' too cold up there about now, so he was more than ready to ride back here with me. What do you care about it, anyway?"

"If he has family," Rose said, "we'll need to notify them. They will want to know."

"We'll take care of that, Sister," Grady said. He had been so quiet, watching Rose and Seth, that his voice startled them.

"No kin," Seth said. "He was all alone. Left a pack of unhappy girls everywhere we stopped, though," he said with a grin. "You might want to tell them if you can find 'em all."

He glanced at Rose as though looking for a reaction. But she was not to be riled again. What she felt most was sadness. Seth had once been a gentle man, full of eager plans for the family farm. With a deep breath, she pushed aside her memories.

"When did you and Johann arrive in Languor?" she asked.

Seth shrugged. "Couple weeks ago or so, I didn't keep careful track."

"He had been with us in North Homage for about two weeks before his death. Did he come directly to us, then?" Rose asked. Grady looked interested.

"I see what you're getting at. Nope, don't see how

anybody in town could have got to know him, leastways not enough to want him dead. He went into town maybe once or twice, and maybe he did meet a girl, but it didn't amount to much." Seth shot a quick glance at a frowning Grady. "Then he just stayed the one night out at the farm, but Pappy couldn't stand him, and he couldn't stand Pappy, and he figured the Shakers would be a good place to find girls." This time his eyes flicked over Gennie.

Rose stiffened. "So your father didn't care for him. What about your brother?"

"My pappy wouldn't kill nobody, and neither would my little brother. They got no reason to kill Johann, hardly knew him." Seth paused over one potato, feeling for soft spots. "Nope, it was one of y'all done it."

Rose counted three deep breaths, her teeth grinding. Sudden distraction came in the form of the sloppily painted sign nailed to the side of Seth's stall. The name astonished her.

"Seth, you're working for Peleg Webster, as well?"

"Yeah?"

"But isn't your father feuding with him?"

"Yup." Seth grinned. "I'm the reason for the feud. The deputy here has just been trying to get me to see if I can stop it, but, well, I don't see why I should."

He swung his full crate onto his hip and heaved it on the back of his wagon. He glanced back at Rose. "Looks like you and me are going to be neighbors for a long time to come."

"Is there somewhere we could speak with you? In private?" Rose asked, when Seth had strolled away to chat with another stall owner.

Grady glanced over his shoulder at the park bench, where the blond girl named Emily still sat. Her Coca-Cola bottle, now empty, balanced on the seat next to her. She watched them with a bored air, her arms folded. One slender leg was crossed over the other and swung rhythmically back and forth, making the red silk of her dress shimmer.

"Let's walk over yonder," he said.

They walked through the market stalls and toward the old kiosk, past a small garden with weeds and one bent, yellow chrysanthemum, seeking the low autumn sun through a thick canopy of trees. Rose shivered inside her heavy cloak. They found an isolated spot under a large sugar maple with glowing red-orange leaves.

"Grady," she said, "it's no use pretending that we won't be blamed for Johann's death. You heard Seth just now. The townspeople will assume it was one of us who killed him."

"Are you so sure they aren't right?" Grady asked.

"Nay, I'm not sure," Rose said slowly. "But I am certain that we can't let things rest as they are. Believe me, the anger will grow. We must know who killed Johann and why. If it was a Believer, then so be it. We abhor violence, you should know that. We will not even fight in a war. For the sake of our community, if we have a murderer in our midst, we must find him out."

"Or her."

"Yea, or her," Rose said, frowning. "So you must see that we are on the same side, you and I. We can help one another."

Grady paused. "I'll tell you this much," he said finally. "Johann had been dead for several days before Gennie found him. He was stabbed through the heart and then buried, likely nearby. Then we figure he was dug up, fresh clothes put on him, and he was moved to the Herb House."

"I guessed as much," Rose said, "after seeing how dirty he was underneath those clean clothes."

"The sheriff thinks Johann never came back to town after going to you all at North Homage," Grady said.

"Can you be certain of that?"

"Well, nobody remembers seeing him after that."

"How hard have you looked? What about that girl Seth says Johann met? Have you located her?"

Grady stared at a point just beyond his toes. "Turned out to be nothing. Anyway, as for the bouquet, the sheriff thinks a Shaker might have done that."

"Why?"

Grady ran a finger inside his shirt collar as if it were too tight. "He thought it could be—well, some ritual or other."

An angry red flush spread across the fair skin of Rose's face. "A *ritual,"* she said in a voice that made both Gennie and Grady step back a pace. "And did he specify what kind of ritual? Never mind, I can guess. Shall we say a 'satanic' ritual? Perhaps he thinks that we routinely murder people, bury them, then dig them up for unspeakable rites."

"Now, Rose, this wasn't my idea. I'm not even sure the sheriff really believes it. And it isn't as bad as it sounds. He just thought that maybe one of you found the body and that there's something you all do to purify, I mean, to chase out evil spirits. Or something," Grady finished lamely.

"Grady O'Neal, you knew that rock was meant for us, didn't you!" Gennie stormed. "That's why that boy called us witches. It isn't only the sheriff who thinks we're evil, everyone in town does. You do, too!"

"No, Gennie, I do not think that of you." This time he took her hands in his and held her eyes. A warmth that was no longer anger shot through her body. She did not pull back.

"Grady," Rose said sharply.

Grady dropped Gennie's hands but neither stepped away nor shifted his gaze.

"All right, Rose," he said. "I guess we are on the same side. I'll try to keep the sheriff's mind open. But I warn you, if a Shaker is involved, don't try to keep it from us."

Rose began to protest that she would never do such a thing, but her words vanished in earsplitting clanging. They spun around to see Languor's ill-equipped fire brigade clamoring past them on the road that Rose and Gennie had traveled from North Homage.

They hurried back toward the market square. Seth leaned against his stall, hands in his pockets, and lazily watched their approach.

"If I was you, Rose," he said, "I'd get back home. There's a rumor going around that the whole place is burning to the ground."

NINE

ROSE AND GENNIE FOLLOWED GRADY'S CAR, BOUNCING at a full fifty miles an hour over the rutted dirt road they had traveled earlier. This time, ragged children and their parents lined the street and stared, but the presence of police discouraged a repeat of the rock-tossing incident.

At first, Rose could see only a billowing cloud of black-gray smoke roll across the sky over North Homage. As they neared the outskirts, the smoke appeared to erupt from a dense, black funnel spiraling upward from the far end of the village.

"Oh, Rose, it's the Herb House," Gennie cried.

"We don't know that yet."

The cars sped right down the unpaved central pathway toward the east end of town. When the path ended just before the wheatfields, they jumped out. Motioning Gennie to stay by the car, Rose stumbled her way through the clumps and ruts of the harvested fields toward the smoke. The blue triangular kerchief that crisscrossed the bodice of her dress worked loose and flopped inside her cape. Her heavy, sugar-scoop bonnet fell back on her neck, and tufts of red hair popped out from under her cotton cap. Panting and disheveled, she reached a group of Believers and police watching the fire brigade. No one chided her for her condition. All eyes were hypnotized by the soaring, spitting flames. It quickly became apparent that the Herb House was unharmed. But a roaring blaze engulfed the barn, which lay just beyond the Herb House.

A familiar odor permeated the air. Rose recognized it from her many visits with the world's people and, more recently, from her encounter with the Camel-smoking police officer. Inside the barn, clumps of curing tobacco leaves had hung from the rafters. The Society's entire tobacco crop smoldered like an enormous cigarette.

Sheriff Brock lounged against an oak tree and surveyed the fire brigade's futile efforts to save the structure. Grady spoke with him briefly and, flipping open his notebook, headed toward a group of onlookers. Seeing Rose approach, Brock strolled back to meet her.

"Did someone set this fire on purpose?" she demanded.

"Looks like it. We already found a couple empty cans of gasoline thrown a few hundred yards away from the barn."

"Now will you believe me that we are in danger?"

Brock lifted his cap, smoothed back his thinning, gray hair, and replaced the cap. "Maybe," he said. "Or maybe a Shaker set this fire."

"What? That's ludicrous. What possible reason could a Believer have for destroying our barn and our entire tobacco crop?"

"I can think of two reasons right offhand," Brock said with a smug nod. "First, look at where that barn is—or was, I should say. Yup, real handy to the Herb House. One idea is that the killer hid something in there, something he couldn't figure out any other way to get rid of. Maybe it was just easier to burn the barn and the evidence than to sneak it out and find another place for it."

The heavy tobacco odor hung on Rose's cloak and stung her eyes. Thick plumes of smoke spiraled into the sky. A sudden crack, and two adjoining wooden walls crumbled into a pile of sparks and cinders. Without their support, the roof caved downward. The falling roof tiles exploded in all directions as they crashed on the ground. The ravenous flames had finally devoured most of their fuel, and they began to subside.

"The way I see it," Brock continued, unmoved by the destruction, "this killer is a real fanatic. He—or she—kills a man who's chasing after Shaker girls, tries to do some strange ritual or other—"

"Sheriff—"

"And maybe a twisted mind like his figured it was justice to burn down the barn while he was trying to hide evidence, what with the barn being full of tobacco and all." Brock squinted in the haze. "Don't it ever seem odd to you that y'all refuse to smoke, but you sell tobacco to the rest of us? A crazy Shaker might just want to put a stop to that, too. That's the way I see it."

Rose turned on her heel and joined the other Believers, who mourned in silence. She was aware, now more than ever, that she'd receive no help from the sheriff, and probably little from Grady. She was on her own.

Gennie dragged her tired legs up the girls' staircase of the Children's Dwelling House, where she lived, stumbling twice over her long skirts. The second time she caught herself with one hand and sat down sharply on a step. Twelve-hour days in the herb fields never made her as tired as she was at that moment. She kicked at the hem of her skirt, still caught on the toe of her shoe, and sighed as she heard the stitching rip. *Elder Wilhelm makes us wear these stupid old dresses,* she thought. *He should have to mend them.*

Gennie heard a door close and children's laughter. She heaved herself up and finished her climb. A crack of light under her retiring room door told her that her roommate, Molly Ferguson, was inside. Gennie was surprised. Molly usually stayed away from the room as late as possible, just to feel some freedom. Often she sat in a rocking chair by a hallway window, watching the grounds, until a sister chased her to bed. With all the excitement this afternoon, she'd have guessed that Molly would be rambling around the village, taking advantage of the lack of supervision.

Gennie knocked lightly and pushed open the door. The room held four beds, all perched on wheels to ease cleaning. No one had slept in two of them for three years, but they remained, waiting for the orphans who rarely came anymore now that there were orphanages to care for them.

Every night, Molly and Gennie pushed their beds to opposite ends of the room, creating an illusion of privacy. They rolled the beds together again each morning, in case a sister walked in during the day and frowned on this yearning. Though she would never tell Rose, Gennie was glad that North Homage had declined in membership from two hundred Believers to thirty. It gave her the chance to be alone now and then.

Molly's narrow bed already hugged the wall. Her roommate sat on her coverlet, her slim legs tucked under her white nightdress. Long, thick hair obscured her face, hair as dark as the cast-iron stove in the center of the room. Without answering Gennie's "Good evening," Molly smoothed a comb through her hair, starting at the nape of her neck and gliding over her head.

Gennie pulled her own bed to the opposite wall, undressed quickly near the stove, and shivered into her nightdress. She had worn the same winter gown for three years. She loved to take it out of storage each fall and feel it pull tighter across her breasts. Something else she couldn't tell Rose. She wriggled under her covers and propped herself on one elbow to watch Molly's bedtime ritual.

Despite her roommate's odd, often distant personality, Gennie felt a kinship with Molly. Both had been placed with the Shakers by a widowed parent who died soon afterward. Gennie had tried to forgive her own father, a dour lawyer who had drawn his strength from her vibrant mother. When she died, so did his will to be a father to Gennie. The Depression's arrival had finally crushed him.

Molly's father had been a construction laborer, whose answer to the Depression was to drink himself to death, forcing Molly and her mother into the streets. Gennie knew little of what happened during that period of Molly's life.

With a flick of her head, Molly tossed her silky hair, and it settled around her shoulders like a soft, dark cloud. She looked at Gennie with half-closed, sulky eyes.

"Ain't you even going to comb that mop?" Molly asked. Her coarse speech was jarring compared with her luxurious looks.

"Nay, what's the use? My hair will never look like yours, even if I comb it all night."

"You got curl. Anyway, you can hide it forever when you become a good little Shaker."

Ignoring the jab, Gennie asked, "Molly, have you ever been in love?"

She began to regret her question as those black eyes laughed at her.

"Did you go and fall in love with a good little Shaker boy?"

"Nay, be serious, Molly. Have you?"

Molly pulled her lustrous hair over one shoulder and absently braided and unbraided it. "Sure, lots of times," she said with a shrug. " 'Course, it never lasted more'n a few hours."

"Oh, honestly, Gen," Molly said, laughing when she saw Gennie's confused frown, "you're such a baby. You don't know nothin'." She sighed. "Heck, I started falling in love when I was fourteen. Learned by watchin' my ma. Me and Ma had to live on the streets after Pa died. At first, we had to knock on back doors and beg for food." Molly's eyes grew even darker at the remembered humiliation. "But then we figured out a better way to get money."

"What was that?"

"Ma would leave me settin' on a park bench," Molly said. "Then she'd go up to some man if he was alone. They'd talk a spell, and then sometimes they'd go off together. See, Ma knew where there was this old, abandoned truck down under a bridge nearby. It was real private. So they'd, you know, fall in love real quick, and she would get some money from the man, and we could rent a room for the night."

Gennie hesitated. She didn't dare ask for too much clarification. Molly would just laugh at her again.

"So," she ventured, "how did you—I mean, when did you fall in love?"

"Fourteen, like I said. I'm tall, so I looked a lot older. And one day, while Ma was off with a man, another one came up to me. He even had a hotel room and everything. He was rich! And I already knew enough to ask for money."

Molly scooted across her bed until her back was against the wall. She straightened her legs and stretched.

"Fallin' in love is easy," she said. "You just gotta know to ask for something back." She pulled her knees up under her chin. " 'Course, my ma figured out pretty fast what I was doing and brought me here. Begged the Shakers to raise me right. Then she went off and died. She should have kept me with her, I could've taken care of her," she said, her voice softer.

Molly flopped over on her stomach. "I'm tired of talking," she said, with a return to her normal hard-edged tone.

"All right, then. Sleep tight." Gennie slipped between her sheets and turned to face the wall. Even under her coverlet, though, she shivered. "I'm going to stoke up the stove a bit," she said, flipping over just in time to see her roommate pull a small object from beneath her thin mattress. Molly slipped her feet under her covers and began to file her nails.

"Molly Ferguson, where did you get that nail file!" Gennie flung off her covers and dashed across the room. "Let me see that," she said, settling on the foot of Molly's bed. "It has mother-of-pearl on the handle. Is it real?"

Molly smiled and nodded. "I got more," she said.

"What? Show me."

Molly considered Gennie for a moment, as though weighing the delight of boasting against the danger of betrayal. Then she reached under her mattress again and came up with two more objects, one shiny and one red. She held them in her curled hand, ready to snatch them back. Gennie leaned over and drew in her breath sharply.

"Is that nail polish? Red nail polish?"

Molly nodded.

"What's the other?"

"Lipstick, silly." Molly popped off the lid and rolled up a mound of bright red. "It's called Ruby."

Gennie thought of Emily, the girl in the red silk dress, the one who must be Grady's girl. Her lips and nails had matched her dress. Molly always did this to her, always brought her near a world that seemed exotic and alluring, just out of reach yet right here in her own room.

"How did you get these? I could never manage it, even if I tried."

"I don't reckon you'd try, would you?" Molly carefully rolled down the lipstick and pushed on the lid.

"I might so," Gennie said, knowing it was a lie. Molly did that to her, too. "Aren't you afraid someone will find them?"

"Who'd find them? We change our own sheets. Nobody's found them yet."

"How did you get all this stuff?"

Molly shrugged. "Someone gave 'em to me."

"Who?"

"None of your business."

"How long have you had them?"

"Near two weeks, and not a peep from anybody. I ain't scared." But she shoved all three items deeply into their hiding place.

A chill skittered down Gennie's spine. Two weeks was just about when Johann Fredericks had arrived in North Homage. Could he have given them to Molly? How well had Molly gotten to know Johann?

Molly straightened again and looked at Gennie's face.

"You better not be thinking about telling, or I'll straighten your hair for you," she said, her dark eyes fierce.

Gennie's sense of foreboding deepened, but not because of Molly's threat. Was there more to Molly's secret than lipstick, nail polish, and a nail file?

"Molly, tell me truly, who gave you those things?"

"Like I said, none of your business, good little Shaker girl." Molly's smile was smug.

Gennie slipped back into her own bed and turned her face to the wall. *The trouble is, Molly's right,* she thought. She wouldn't try to get lipstick or nail polish, and she wouldn't know anyone who could get them for her. She brooded that maybe she was destined to be a Shaker sister. If she could be like Rose, of course, it wouldn't be so bad. Rose always knew what to do and what to say. She did easily everything that was so difficult for Gennie. Maybe if she worked very, very hard, she could be like that someday? Nay, that was impossible, of course. Everything that Rose said and did grew out of her love for the Society, her complete devotion to its beliefs. Deep in her heart, Gennie felt little of that in herself.

She closed her eyes and conjured the image of her mother's face—not as she was during the last few weeks of her life, losing weight, losing strength, but the laughing mother with auburn curls, like Gennie's, but piled whimsically on her head. Did she always laugh? Gennie neither remembered nor cared. All she remembered was the laughter. But for some reason it brought tears to her eyes. She reached under her pillow for her handkerchief, trying not to sniffle.

Molly heard, though.

"Gen? You all right?"

Gennie opened her eyes to darkness.

"I didn't mean to make you cry," Molly said softly.

Gennie heard Molly's bed squeak as she sat up.

"I'll tell you a secret," Molly whispered, "but you gotta promise not to tell, cross your heart and hope to die."

Gennie's eyes had adjusted to the dark, and she saw Molly swing her legs over the side of her bed.

"What is it?" Gennie asked brusquely, uncertain whether Molly meant to be kind or to ridicule her again.

"First, promise."

"All right, I promise."

Molly hesitated a moment, then left her bed for Gennie's. Gennie sat up and pulled her knees under her chin, squinting to see Molly's face in the dark.

"I wore the lipstick outside," Molly whispered, leaning forward.

"I don't believe you. You'd have been caught. No Shaker girl could wear red lipstick in broad daylight and not be seen by a dozen sisters."

"Maybe it wasn't daylight."

Gennie could hear the smirk in her voice.

"Nay, you couldn't have gone out at night. I'd have heard you."

"You? Once you're asleep, you wouldn't hear a freight train if it ran over your bed."

Molly was right, she did sleep soundly.

Molly reached across the dark and grabbed Gennie's

hands. "Promise again you won't tell nobody." As Molly drew close, a sweet scent brushed the air.

Has someone given her perfume, as well? Gennie wondered. But it could just be the lavender rinse used in the laundry. Gennie said simply, "Yea, I promise."

Molly released Gennie's hands and clasped her arms around her legs. Both girls shivered with the chill air and the excitement of secrets about to be shared.

"I wore the lipstick for a man," Molly whispered, "and the nail polish, too." She giggled like the young girl she still was. "He liked them, too. He said I was beautiful. He said he would kiss the lipstick off my lips. He did, too, he kissed me and kissed me."

Now that she had begun to reveal her secret, the words tumbled out. Gennie kept very still.

"He did other things, too, after a while." She giggled again. "We went into the Water House 'cause it was too cold outside. It was cold in the Water House, too. That was the only part I didn't like. He spread my cloak on that dirty old floor, and then he touched me a lot, all over. And then . . . well, you know." Molly laughed knowingly. When she spoke again, her voice was thoughtful. "Mama said it wasn't fun, just something a woman's gotta put up with to get a roof over her head. But that time I liked it."

Gennie was glad for the darkness. Her cheeks felt hot with the humiliation of ignorance. She did not know what Molly had done with this nameless man. No one, not even Rose, had told her just what a man and a woman did together, except that it was sinful and best not contemplated.

"Who did you meet? Not one of the brethren, surely."

Molly whooped at the thought, and the sound seemed to fill the large room. "Can you imagine me and old Brother Hugo in the Water House?"

"Shush," Gennie whispered urgently. "You'll have Sister Charlotte here checking on us."

Molly kept giggling, but more quietly. At the sound of a door closing nearby, she rushed to her own bed. Both girls lay still, listening for footsteps and a chiding voice, but none came.

"You know," Molly whispered, "right after I got dumped here, I asked Charity if she thought my ma was right—you know, about it not being any fun with men." Molly laughed softly. "She turned red as my lipstick and said it was an awful sin and don't even think about it. But I know she thought about it as much as me." Molly's bed creaked as she settled under the covers.

"How do you know?" Gennie asked.

"Because she wanted him, too." Molly's voice was fading. "But I got him first."

Gennie's mind flipped back to the Union Meeting the previous Thursday, the one she had described to Sheriff Brock and Grady O'Neal. Charity and Johann exchanging a forbidden special look, Charity blushing . . . Gennie lay very still, her inner confusion forgotten, her fears confirmed. The man Molly had met was Johann Fredericks, and Gennie had just promised not ever to tell.

TEN

THE FIRST SHAFTS OF GOLDEN DAWN WARMED HER oak desk as Rose chewed the tip of her pen. For a moment, she could not bear to reread her work, a summary of what she had learned from the previous late-afternoon and evening's questioning of fifteen of North Homage's thirty Believers about Johann Fredericks and about the fire which had destroyed their barn. No one offered information about the fire, but several had a great deal to say about Johann and who he'd had dealings with.

She had arisen at 4:00, an hour early for a Saturday, and padded in slippered feet downstairs to her office to complete her task. Rather than add scarce wood to the stove, merely for her own comfort, she had wrapped herself in her thick wool cloak and kept her chilled feet under its long folds. She longed for a steaming pot of rose hip and lemon balm tea, but she hadn't wanted to clatter crockery in the kitchen at such an early hour.

Rose yawned and stretched her arms, then shivered as the cloak slid from her lap. She replaced it quickly. Her eyes fell on the sheet of paper before her, but still she resisted reading it. A glance around the dimly lit room filled her with sadness and rare loneliness. A hundred years ago, the Trustees' Office, the building in which Rose lived and worked, would have been filled with people. She would have been one of four trustees, two men and two women, who met daily with the world's folk in this very room.

Though small by Shaker standards, the building contained retiring rooms for fifty Believers, sisters housed on the west side, brethren on the east, each with their own staircase. The staircases had a simple elegance, though they were not as exquisite as the curved ones Rose had seen as a child on a visit to the Trustees' Office in the Pleasant Hill Shaker village, before it closed in 1910.

Now Rose shared the building with only two others, young novitiates who had not yet signed the covenant to become full members of the Society. They were good girls, eager and hardworking, but they couldn't fill the large house with the bustle and cheerful noise of fifty Believers.

Since Sister Fiona's death last spring, Rose was the last remaining trustee, working alone to direct the business affairs of North Homage. She reached out and smoothed her hand across Fee's half of the double desk, then drew back into the warmth of her cape. The pigeonholes still held Fee's old accounts books and postal supplies, as though she would pop in at any moment to fill out invoices for herb orders.

What would Fee have to say about her list of potential Shaker murderers? Something plainspoken, no doubt, she thought, smiling. Fee's parents had brought her from Ireland almost directly to North Homage when she was a small child. Some of Fee's first memories had been of the Civil War, when both Union and Confederate soldiers marched through North Homage demanding food and horses. Rose remembered the stories as though Fee sat beside her now telling them, her small body ramrod-straight and her eyes bright.

"They were starving, the poor lads," Fee had reminisced more than once, "and we fed them good Shaker meals, with cheese, applesauce, brown bread and butter, lemon pie, even roasted chickens if we had them. We went without to feed them. But when they wanted our brethren to come and fight, we stood firm. We Shakers do not fight. We do not kill. Even when our neighbors stole our horses to punish us for not fighting, we showed them no anger in return. Remember that, Rose, take no revenge on those who would be your enemies." Then with a wink, "Not so easy for an Irish lass, is it?"

Shakers do not kill. Rose pulled her list toward her. Fourteen Believers remained to be questioned. She eliminated seven Believers who were too elderly or ill even to leave their retiring rooms. Another two were traveling from town to town in northern Kentucky, selling Shaker products. That left Eldress Agatha and the four names that popped up over and over. Those four she planned to question this morning.

Nearly everyone she had questioned so far knew who Johann was, and most swore that they'd avoided contact with him. But several had witnessed extended, sometimes angry, interchanges between the dead man and Albert Preston, Elder Wilhelm Lundel, and Sister Elsa Pike. Because of the special look they'd exchanged at the Union Meeting, Rose added Sister Charity McDonald's name to the list. Off to the side, she wrote Seth Pike, with a question mark. He'd said they were friends, yet no one had ever seen them together. Had they had a falling-out? Beneath Seth's name, she added a question about the girl Johann had met in town and her connection with Grady.

The sooner she questioned all of the people on her list, the better for North Homage. Any moment, Sheriff Brock might reappear and begin his own brand of interrogation, designed to find a Shaker killer. And the angry outsiders—she wanted to believe it was outsiders—who had destroyed their barn might strike again and again, until the killer was found and brought to justice. If the killer were a Believer, what would be the world's reaction then? She wouldn't think too much about that. Justice was their only chance.

The large dining room held two clusters of empty tables and benches, one for the sisters and the other for the brethren, separated by a wide expanse of open floor. The sweet, spicy smell of baking apple pies drifted in from the kitchen.

Charity McDonald slid onto one of the sisters' benches and shifted her knees under the table, her wide eyes fixed on Rose's face. Charity's normally fair skin was almost colorless. Rose gave her a reassuring smile and circled the table to sit opposite her.

"Charity, there is no need to be frightened, truly," Rose said firmly—and, she hoped, accurately. Charity seemed to bring out protective feelings in all the sisters—except Elsa, that is. Perhaps it was those doelike eyes. That, and an emotional frailty made her seem unable to thrive on her own, without the strength of the Society. As long as her position was secure within the community, she was able to contribute her part, even performing adequately as kitchen deaconess. But Rose imagined that any fear of being cast out might result in Charity's disintegration.

"You're here to ask about that man, aren't you? I did not know him, not really," Charity said in a soft, little-girl voice. "We only greeted one another a few times on the road outside the Meeting House and when I served him during meals, but . . ." Charity shifted her gaze away from Rose and to her own lap, where she intertwined her fingers so tightly that the knuckles whitened.

Rose noted the clenched hands and averted gaze and sensed Charity was hiding something, perhaps even lying. In her dealings with the world's merchants, Rose had found that careful silence and a steady gaze often flustered those who were trying to cheat her. More often than not, they backed down and, in the end, treated her fairly. So she let the silence weigh on Charity's conscience. It took only a few seconds.

"We only talked about the weather and the apple harvests, that's all, truly," Charity said. But her face puckered and her breath grew ragged.

"Charity, no one accuses you, but you must see how important this is. Someone has taken the life of another human being. That is terrible enough to any Believer, but the police are eager to blame one of us. So we have to search for Johann's killer on our own, and to do that, we must know him, what he was like, how he treated you as well as others. We must have the whole truth from everyone."

Charity nodded faintly and pulled a handkerchief from her sleeve to dab at the tears spilling from her eyes. She took a deep, jerky breath.

"I didn't mean for it to happen," she said in a hushed voice. "It was after dinner one night a few days before Johann was . . . before he disappeared. I was cleaning up in the kitchen and splashed a pan full of water down the front of my dress." She glanced ruefully down at the neckerchief crossed over her bodice, which showed sticky drips of apple pie filling. "I was soaked clear through, so I told Elsa to keep cleaning while I went to my retiring room to change into dry clothing. It was dusk and no one was about and . . . Johann just seemed to appear out of nowhere. He was holding a pink rose, and he handed it to me. He said I should wear it in my hair." Charity's cheeks reddened, and Rose wondered again if she were telling everything. "I gave the flower right back to him, I assure you. I told him that we Believers do not adorn ourselves with flowers." Her pride steadied her voice.

"And what did he say to that?" Rose prompted.

"Oh, not much." Charity shrugged, and stared over Rose's shoulder out the dining-room window.

"What exactly did he say and do?"

"I've told you all there is. He just left."

Could Johann have frightened her so that she feared him even after his death? *Nay,* Rose thought, *more likely she fears losing her place in the Society.* The best course would be to let it go for now and talk to her again later, reassure her that her transgression can be forgiven and forgotten. Unless it was murder, of course.

Sister Elsa Pike marched into the dining room on sturdy, determined legs. She faced Rose with flour-covered hands on her broad hips, her mouth hardened into a grim line.

"I got work to do," she said.

"And you'll be back to it soon enough."

"If it's about that Johann, all I can say is, he got what he deserved, and I don't care who knows it, but him and me had nothing to do with each other. Anybody says anything else is a liar." Her eyes narrowed to pencil-thin lines to match her mouth.

Rose felt her own jaw tighten for a fight. "You may want to believe that, Elsa, but the fact is that no fewer than four Believers told me that they saw you—"

The west door of the dining room slammed behind her. She twisted on her bench to find Brock and Grady bearing down on her.

"Well now, that's mighty interesting," Brock said, grinning. "You want to tell us what four Shakers saw Elsa Pike doing, Miss Callahan? Write this down, Grady."

So much for her private interrogations, Rose thought. Elsa, however, saved her from the need to respond instantly.

"Harry Brock, you ought to be ashamed of yerself!" Elsa bellowed. "I mean, thee," she added, at a lower decibel level. Brock grinned at her.

"Wipe that grin off thy face. I knowed thee since you was a kid, Harry Brock, and you got no call to accuse me of killin' a man. Heck, if I didn't kill that no-good husband of mine when I had the chance, I sure wouldn't kill nobody now I'm a Believer." She thrust out a plump, defiant chin. "I got a good life here. I got a religion."

"Yeah, well, if you've known me, then remember, I've known you, too. I know a whole lot about you, Elsa Pike. So stop yammering and tell me what you know about Johann Fredericks."

Elsa plunked herself down on a dining-room bench, brushing bits of flour and dough from her dress.

"All right, all right. I know'd a lot about Mr. Johann Fredericks," she said, with a mixture of scorn and relish. "I'm more worldly than most Shaker gals, ya know. So I know his type." She gave a satisfied nod. "He was after the girls, I could see that a mile off. Even went after that one, that Sister Charity." She jerked her head toward the kitchen. "Don't ask me why, skinny little thing, no spunk." She patted her own ample stomach and smiled.

"You got that name, Grady?" Brock asked.

"It was wise of you to want to protect the sisters," Rose said quickly. "Did you by any chance try to speak to Johann about his behavior?"

"You bet I did!" For the moment, Elsa gave up her attempt to transform her vernacular into gentle Shaker language. "I gave that boy what-for, 'specially when I caught him going after the young'uns, like that Molly, though I can't say as how she didn't give him ideas. She's the type needs watchin'. Saw 'em talkin' together in the apple orchard. I'd gone there to pray after supper," Elsa said, with a pious tilt of her head.

"What's this Molly's full name, Elsa?" Brock asked.

"Ferguson, Molly Ferguson, no more'n seventeen and wild as they come."

Rose's heart sank. She should have moved much

more quickly. Brock would have his Shaker villain in no time. She mentally added Molly's name to her list.

"When was this that you saw the deceased and this girl together?" Brock asked.

"That Thursday night, the night he disappeared. I remember thinkin' I had to git back for the Union Meetin'. Couldn't hear what they was sayin'," Elsa said, with evident regret. "But they was arguin', clear enough. I know what arguin' is, sure did it enough with that no-good husband of mine."

"And you spoke with Johann after this incident?" Rose asked.

"Yup! I mean, yea, I did. Molly run off toward the Meetin' House, so I went and told Johann to leave her and the other girls alone. I put the fear of God in that boy by the time I was done with him!"

Elsa could certainly reduce Charity to tears, but not a man like Johann. Rose suspected he would merely have laughed at Elsa.

"Did you discuss anything else?"

Was it her imagination, or did Elsa seem hesitant? Unlike Charity, Elsa showed no outward signs of nervousness. But she gave her answer a few moments' thought, which was rare for her.

"Wouldn't have no cause to discuss the weather after all that, would I now?"

Rose silently studied her, as she had Charity, but Elsa was woven from tougher thread. She met Rose's inquiring gaze with steady eyes and complete silence.

"What about Molly? Did you speak to her about her meeting with Johann?" Rose asked.

"Yup, found her right before the Meetin'. I pulled her round back of the Meetin' House and give her a talkin'-to she won't soon forgit. She'd of been my child, she'd still be too sore to set down."

"You didn't strike her, did you?"

"'Course not! I know better'n that, now I'm a Believer. Besides," she added with a snort, "never did no good for my own boys. They always did just what they wanted, 'specially that Seth, bringin' that no-good Johann back with him."

This was a direction Rose did not wish to take, not now, in front of Brock and Grady. She had hoped to talk to Elsa privately about her eldest son and how well he had gotten along with Johann. But if she didn't ask now, the sheriff would.

"Elsa, about Seth," Rose began. "We know that he and Johann rode the rails together and that Seth brought him to your . . . his father's farm. And we think there was a falling-out of some sort just before Johann moved in here with us. What can you tell us about that?"

As Rose spoke, Elsa's body stiffened, her face tightening into a grim mask.

"You got no call to accuse my son of nothing. You of all people. Oh, I know all about you, Sister High an' Mighty, don't think I don't. I had eyes in my head, and—"

"Elsa," Rose interrupted sharply, "we must know about everyone who knew Johann. Everyone. That includes Seth." Rose felt the sheriff's eyes on her, but she focused on Elsa's face, schooling herself to notice the slightest twitch or blush. And there were many, as every weatherworn line seemed in perpetual motion.

"Seth's had some hard times, but he's a good boy at heart. He *is.*" Elsa's normally flat features twisted into fierce mother love. "He's got a load of anger in him and maybe it shows too much, but he ain't no killer. Why, when he was maybe fourteen, we had a workhorse get sick, and his pa wanted him to shoot it, and Seth couldn't do it. Couldn't even shoot a sick horse. His pa give him a swat with his belt, buckle an' all, but Seth, he just walked away. Stayed mad at his pa for weeks and weeks, but he never did shoot that horse. He ain't no killer. His pa, now there's a killer." Elsa's face brightened at the idea of blaming her husband for

Johann's murder. "Shot that horse without a second thought. Always went around sayin' he was gonna shoot the neighbors' horses if they stepped on our land, and maybe the neighbors, too."

Brock jumped in. "You suggesting he got hisself over here at night and killed a strapping young man like Johann? Poor Billy's a cripple, you know that, Elsa."

"Poor Billy? Ha! It's God's judgment on him, him bein' lame, you can bet on that. The way he run around. Always cheatin' on me with any woman from fifty miles around. Makes sense, don't it, that God took away his legs?"

"Well, now, Elsa," Brock said in that easygoing tone that Rose had learned to fear. "That's not quite how I heared it. The way I heared it, Billy ain't the only one was cheatin' in your family."

Elsa gripped the edge of the table and stiffened as though waiting for a blow.

"So tell me, Elsa," Brock said. "Just who is Seth's pappy?"

The ruddiness in Elsa's face drained away, leaving only her fierce hazel eyes for color. For once, she had nothing to say.

ELEVEN

"WE'LL TALK TO THOSE TWO GIRLS, CHARITY AND Molly, later," Sheriff Brock grumbled after allowing a grim and unresponsive Elsa to return to her kitchen duties. "But first, we got some questions for you and this Wilhelm Lundel."

Brock and Grady now sat in Rose's office, where she should have felt more in command, but even in these cozy surroundings, the sheriff kept her off-balance.

"Why me?"

"Seems like this Johann was quite a ladies' man. I know how y'all feel about that sort of thing. Now, you claim you never spoke to him, but I was wondering, you sure you wasn't one of the sisters the deceased got too fresh with, Miss Callahan?"

"No, I most certainly was not!" Rose bristled. "When you know us better, you'll understand how insulting these questions are. I am a Believer. Do you understand what that means to me? It means that I worship God in my every act, my thoughts, in all that I am. When I do business with a merchant from the world, I am always honest because my work is worship. That chair you're sitting in, feel the tight weave of the seat, the slight angle of the back, how comfortable and practical it is. Each chair is made with such care. And why? Because it is an act of worship. Nay, Sheriff, I do not lie. If I say that I never spoke with Johann Fredericks, then I did not."

Without pausing, Rose sprang from her chair and unhooked her cloak from one of the wooden pegs lining the wall.

"We'll speak with Elder Wilhelm," she said as she tied the cloak across her shoulders and covered her light gauze cap with a stiffly woven bonnet. "He is harvesting apples this morning, but we can ask him to leave his work briefly." She stood straight and tall, her chin squared in what Fiona used to call her no-nonsense pose.

The men rose slowly to their feet, Grady watching Sheriff Brock, and Brock watching Rose. There was a look in his eyes that Rose hoped was respect. But she did not delude herself. She needed to work fast.

"All right, you win, Miss Callahan," Brock said, reaching for the hat he had thrown on her desk rather than hang it on a peg. "I reckon you're truthful. Leastways, Grady seems to think you can be trusted." He shot a glance at Grady, who stared at the floor. "But we'll see about the others."

Located across the village from the Trustees' Office, the declining orchard delighted both children and adults. Once a lush ten acres, now the shrinking community could maintain only five acres with straight rows of apple trees. The less predictable peaches and plums had succumbed to disease and drought. Dead or feeble trees lined the outermost end, but these were hidden from anyone approaching the orchard from the village, the direction Rose, Brock, and Grady followed.

Elder Wilhelm balanced on a low ladder under an apple tree, his muscular arm yanking the ripe fruits and tossing them into a basket crooked over his free arm. When Rose called his name, he peered down through the branches, his face puckered with irritation.

"What is it? I don't have time to waste."

"If you would be so good as to give us a few moments . . ." Rose said with a slight movement of her head to indicate visitors behind her.

Wilhelm frowned at Brock and Grady. With a loud sigh, he descended the ladder in two long steps. Swinging his basket to the ground, he folded his arms across his broad chest. He stared down at the smaller Brock with a look that Rose had seen many times and which usually sent its recipient a step or two backwards. Brock stood his ground and returned the stare.

"Well?"

"We have a few questions for you," Brock said in a conversational tone. "Likely you'll want to come a ways out of here to talk," he suggested, sweeping his arm toward the open field beyond the orchard.

Wilhelm hesitated. But the voices of nearby Believers seemed to convince him, and he silently led the way through the trees to a freshly harvested field dark with loose, muddy soil. Outside the protection of the orchard, a biting wind whipped their clothing.

"Is thy work done for the day, Sister?" Wilhelm said.

Rose willed her feet to stay where they were. She was not immune to Wilhelm's stern power, but she wouldn't be cowed. Anyway, she was irritated with him for calling her Sister only and not Rose. Shakers usually called each other by their first names, no matter what their positions in the Society. By refusing to do so, Wilhelm flaunted his superior rank.

"This is my work just now, Wilhelm," she said evenly.

"Am I a suspect in this murder, then?"

"Now, no one's callin' you a suspect," Brock said almost jovially. "Leastways, not yet."

"All right, but be quick about it. We haven't enough able-bodied workers to get the apple crop in as it is. Ask thy questions, Sheriff."

Brock had a satisfied-cat look, his bright eyes half-lidded and a faint smile curving his lips. Rose was beginning to understand that beneath his drawl was a shrewd mind intent on getting what he wanted from each person he questioned, no matter how formidable.

The sheriff shoved his hands into his jacket pockets. "Well, now, Mr. Lundel, seeing as how you knew the deceased—I'm not sayin' you knew him more'n to speak to, mind you—but I'm thinkin' you could tell us about him."

"Tell what?" Wilhelm's own hands must be stinging with the cold, but he kept them stiff at his side.

"Would you say Fredericks was, well, a respectful guest in your community?" Brock's face showed only curiosity.

Wilhelm hesitated, the muscles in his jaw working visibly.

"Nay," he answered briskly, "Johann Fredericks was not respectful of our beliefs. He pretended to be, even talked about joining us. He asked many questions about our beliefs and about us ourselves. Who we were, where we came from, where our other communities are located. But he was only collecting information for his own purposes. I soon saw what he was."

"And what was that, Mr. Lundel?"

Wilhelm stared at the empty field, his back straight and proud, his shoulders squared. Rose had often been struck by his military bearing, so unexpected in a pacifist Shaker. He had come to the Society as an adult and had confessed to the elder, rather than to the whole community during worship. Was he a former military man? Had those muscular arms carried a weapon at one time, even injured or killed another human being? Whatever his past, knowledge of it had died with the late elder.

Wilhelm's voice, when he finally spoke, was slow and precise, as though he weighed and measured every word before uttering it.

"Johann Fredericks was . . . a disappointment. He

wanted to use us. As do many others." Wilhelm paused for a long moment. Sheriff Brock, head tilted to the side, watched him steadily. Grady held his stubby pencil poised over his small notebook.

"Look at this field," Wilhelm said with sudden force. He flung his arms wide as though embracing the land. "The winter wheat ought to be planted by now, and we've barely prepared the soil. Once this field and hundreds of acres more besides were filled with long, straight rows. There were no complaints about too much work. We brethren sang as we finished the harvest. The sisters brought us food as we worked the long days and evenings, and sometimes they joined us to work in the fields. We raced to see who could do the quickest and best work and then shared in the pleasure of each other's success."

Wilhelm raised his arms skyward, exhorting a field full of spellbound Believers only he could see. Rose scanned the empty landscape and knew that the vision Wilhelm described was one he himself could never have experienced.

North Homage, facing rapid declines in membership and the devastation of the Civil War, had sold much of its acreage nearly sixty-five years ago. Five years before Wilhelm's birth. And the scenes of intense productivity he described went back in time even farther—to the first half of the nineteenth century, when new Believers signed the covenant almost daily, often entire families at a time. *He wants to duplicate the days of glory that he sees in his mind,* Rose thought. *He has even convinced himself that he was part of that history.*

Wilhelm dropped his arms suddenly. "Johann was a disappointment because he could not really understand us, though he said he wanted to join us. He could never live as a Believer."

"Couldn't live without the ladies, you mean?"

Wilhelm's lip curled with disgust. "He was a fornicator, a damned fornicator." He closed his eyes and filled his lungs with air.

"He had no real call to be one of us," he continued, more quietly. "A Believer must be willing to work hard, and Johann—nay, he could not be bothered to work. It might interfere with his . . . other activities."

Frowning, Brock kicked at a clod of dirt.

"Is it thy belief," Wilhelm asked, "that I would kill a man, break my own sacred vows, just because Johann would have made a bad Believer?"

The dirt broke apart against his toe, and Brock squinted up at Wilhelm.

"I don't know much about your ways," he said slowly. "Tell me, what do you all do when a Shaker dies?"

Wilhelm's forehead furrowed in puzzlement, and Rose held her breath.

"When a Believer dies, we bury him, Sheriff," Wilhelm said. "What do thy people do?"

A broad smile spread across Brock's face. "Same thing, Mr. Lundel, same thing. But, well, we'd have a little ceremony. You know, a service. Maybe we'd say some special prayers. Over to St. Mary's, they might sprinkle a little Holy Water, something like that."

"Ah. We have a simple service, of course."

Brock opened his mouth again, but Wilhelm continued, "And the answer to thy next question is 'nay,' we do not cover the body with herbs. We do not use flowers or herbs for ornament, only for practical purposes, for food or medicine. Johann no longer had need of either."

"Now some religions," Brock continued, "they do even more if the circumstances are what you might call unusual. Some folks even have a ceremony they do for getting rid of evil spirits and such like. Ever heard of such a thing, Mr. Lundel?"

"I believe it is called an exorcism," Wilhelm said. "But I do not think that it is performed at a funeral."

Rose had to force herself to breathe. There was so much in Shaker history that could seem sinister to someone from the world. How truly ignorant was Brock about their past? Was he using his knowledge to trap Wilhelm—any of them, for that matter—by twisting their words and their beliefs? One hundred years earlier, in the 1830s, it was common for Believers to have visions and messages from the dead. It was common in the outside world, too, but no one would remember that. The Shakers have strange ceremonies surrounding the dead, that's all anyone would remember.

"Ever done an exorcism yourself, Mr. Lundel?"

"Nay, Sheriff, never. We do not conduct such ceremonies. I have books that would help thee to understand us better. But I can assure thee that Johann Fredericks was not subjected to any type of ritual by me or any other Believer."

Brock nodded slowly.

"And now, Sheriff, if our interview is finished, I have work to do, and I am losing precious daylight."

"Just one more thing, Mr. Lundel, and then we're done for now. Were y'all planning to open up your Sunday meeting to the public, like you been doing?"

"Yea, as always," Wilhelm said with a tight-lipped smile. "Is it thy wish to join us?"

The sheriff did not smile in return. If anything, he looked more serious than he had throughout the entire interview.

"I'm hopin' you'll change your mind," he said. "None of my business, maybe, but—"

"Correct, Sheriff Brock, it is not thy concern."

"What I'm sayin' is, it'd be better for everyone if you'd keep to yourselves tomorrow. From what I hear, them services of yours is gettin' to be real popular entertainment, and right now y'all ain't so popular yourselves. If something was to happen tomorrow, there ain't much I could do about it. All I got is Grady here and one other officer, and we're mostly tied up with something else. We can't help you keep everything peaceful. Not right now."

"We do not need thy help."

The sharpness in Wilhelm's tone surprised Rose. He had seemed to be in calm control when the sheriff hinted at mysterious Shaker rituals for the dead, but now he reacted with quick anger to a simple request to close the worship service to the public. There was certainly a precedent for closing the service, as Rose well knew. During dangerous, unsettled times in the past, the Society had closed its Meetinghouse doors and worshiped away from the hostile eyes of the world's people. Often, they canceled Sunday services altogether if the harvest was at a critical point, as Wilhelm claimed it was. *So why,* Rose wondered, *is Wilhelm so determined to hold a public worship service, now of all times?*

TWELVE

"MOLLY IS DOING HER ROTATION ON LAUNDRY, SHERiff. She'll be upstairs." Rose had to raise her voice to be heard over the pounding of the agitators in the huge washing machines lining the wall of the dimly lit ground-floor laundry room. Two sisters piled clean, wet clothing into a large basket set on a wooden platform attached to a hoist. When the basket was full, the sisters pulled it upward through a hole in the ceiling. Grady and Brock watched, mesmerized, as the basket traveled to the floor above. The sisters flashed amused smiles at Rose and curious glances at the men without slowing the pace of their work.

"Pretty fancy," Brock said. "I thought you folks were supposed to be such hard workers. What's wrong with carrying your clothes upstairs the normal way?"

"Our faith requires that we work hard," Rose responded, "not that we break our backs. We've always invented labor-saving devices to make our work quicker and better. It leaves more time for worship."

"Yeah?"

They reached the plain, wooden staircase in the center of the room. Rose climbed a few steps before pausing to point to the row of washing machines.

"Those agitators, for example," she said. "They make laundering far more efficient. A Believer invented that."

"I never heard that," Brock said, his eyebrows shooting upward. "Y'all take out a patent?"

"Life is hard enough," Rose said. "We prefer to share our discoveries with the world. We usually don't bother with patents."

"So you can't prove anything, can you?"

Rose let the question hang. She decided not to push the matter further by listing Believers' other inventions, such as the clothespin and the circular saw. It would only make him combative and probably tougher on Molly.

Rose led the group upstairs to a large, bright room cluttered with clothes and ironing boards. Tall, narrow, oak panels with long handles lined one wall. Molly stood before one of the panels, both hands grasping the handle. With the easy strength of youth, she slid the panel straight out from the wall to reveal long rows of linen napkins and pillowcases draped smoothly over rods attached to the back of the panel. Rose was proud of this feature, an adaptation of the steam-drying laundry in the Canterbury, New Hampshire, Shaker community. The clothes dried quickly, needed little ironing, and the whole process was neatly out of sight. It pleased Rose's sense of order and efficiency.

For the moment, Molly fit the picture well. She gave no more than a quick, disinterested glance at the visitors, lingering a moment on Grady, then attended to her task with apparent concentration. She smoothed the hem of a napkin between her fingers, testing for dryness. Satisfied, she folded it with a swift movement and placed it in one of several baskets. But discontent clouded her lovely face. Her full lips, though still sensuous, were pulled into a frown. Her dark eyes locked on the laundered items as if she were alone with them. Only the studied grace of her movements hinted at her awareness that two men watched her.

"Molly," Rose began, "we must speak with you.

Would you prefer to go outside?" She touched the girl's arm gently.

Molly's dusky, unreadable eyes met Rose's for an instant. She shrugged her slender shoulders and wordlessly led the group to the wall where the drying-rack panels ended, farther from the well-meaning but curious ears of the other two sisters. With the washing machines pounding downstairs and the hiss of steam piped to the drying racks, there was little danger of being overheard.

Though the sheriff and Grady had by now learned to keep their distance from Shaker women and girls, Rose stood protectively between them and Molly. She was surprised by her mothering instincts, usually elicited only by Gennie and which the gypsylike Molly was unlikely to appreciate.

Molly leaned a shoulder against the wall and pushed her hip outward into an alluring curve.

Brock paced back and forth before Rose and Molly, jangling some keys in his pockets. He stopped in front of Molly. She met his stare with defiance.

"You might as well tell us everything, you know," Brock said. "We got enough information to put two and two together and get plenty. You're just a kid. Spill it all now, we'll go easy on you."

Molly watched him in silence, but her lip trembled slightly. Rose knew she should want Molly to be truthful, but instead she found herself hoping the child would stay quiet.

"Well?" Brock demanded.

Molly shrugged. "Can't help you if I don't know what you're talking about."

Brock's eyes narrowed to a slit. He jangled his keys again in a rhythmic way.

"We know you and Johann Fredericks was keeping company," he said. "We know you had a falling-out, and next thing anybody knows, the man is dead."

Molly crossed her arms and hugged herself hard. "What of it?"

"What went on between you two?"

"Can't recall." Her eyes were wide and watchful under their dark lashes.

"Not good enough. We know you two argued. What about?"

"Nothin'. Weren't no argument, anyways. We was just talkin'. I ain't no Shaker yet, you know. Ain't likely to be, neither." She tossed her head, which would have been more effective had her long, black hair not been tightly contained in her white, gauze cap.

"Girl, you was *seen* arguing with Johann," Brock continued, his voice now clipped and firm.

Molly raised her free shoulder in a sulky shrug. "Reckon he got a little fresh, and I had to put him in his place. Men do, ya know."

"You're lyin', girl," Brock snapped. "You was seen in a big fight with the man, and clingin' on him, too. Sounds more like you was throwin' yourself at him."

"I was not!"

"Well, I think you done just that," Brock said, poking a finger at Molly's face. "I think he was the one who put *you* in *your* place. And you didn't like it none, did you?"

"That's a lie! You can't say that to me. Rose, make him stop!"

Rose closed her eyes briefly and made a prayerful request for patience. Brock had a certain cunning, but his bullying treatment of women and girls could only backfire in a Shaker community, where Believers consider women equal to men because they see God, thought bodiless in human terms, as possessing both male and female attributes. Rose supposed she could try to explain this to the sheriff, but he would never understand, and surely he could not change. Rose wished for privacy and the leisure to lead Molly gently out of her lie and into the truth, but now she had to do something fast. Brock would soon have Molly incriminating herself. She turned to Brock.

"Sheriff, Molly has been working since sunup, she's tired. I can't allow her to be questioned further now." Rose forced herself to soften her voice. "Besides, we'll all work better on a full stomach. We eat on a regular schedule here, and it is time for our noon meal. Would you and Deputy O'Neal join us? We always have food enough for guests. Our only request is that you will sit with the brethren and remain silent during the meal." She smiled and waved her arm toward the stairs. "I believe I smelled apple pie from the dining room."

Brock glared at Molly for a few seconds, then said gruffly, "Guess we could all do with a bite. But don't you wander off, girl," he said, pointing a warning finger at Molly. "I got a lot to ask you."

Gennie carried a tureen of steaming potato soup to the brethren's side of the dining room and saw Grady O'Neal sitting at the end of one bench, next to Sheriff Brock. Grady saw her come toward him, started to rise as though to help her, then sat down again at a word from one of the brethren. Gennie understood. If he had taken the tureen from her hands, he might have brushed against her accidentally. But he did smile at her, just a little. Gennie met his eyes without daring to smile back.

On her return to the kitchen, Gennie glanced over at the sisters' table and noticed Rose and Molly sitting together. They sat in silence, as did all the sisters. Rose's thin, pale face was composed, Gennie guessed, in prayer. She seemed unaware of Molly's constant movement and restless eyes, which sought out the two policemen across the room. Had Molly told them of her rendezvous with Johann, and did they now suspect her of murder? Why else would Rose sit protectively next to her, still deep in prayer while the soup in front of her grew cold?

In the kitchen, the warm air, yeasty and sweet with fresh bread and apple pie, could not dispel the continuing chill between its occupants.

"Elsa, don't cut the bread so thickly," Charity snapped, as she scraped hunks of butter onto small dishes. For once she had remembered to wear an apron, and already it was streaked with potato soup.

"Won't need no bread if you waste the butter like that," Elsa retorted, hacking at thick brown bread with more vigor than was usual for a nonviolent Shaker sister. Her strong arms embedded the knife in the wood cutting board with each whack. With a grin at Charity's back, Elsa sliced a few extra-thick pieces. She scooped up the slices in her broad, stubby hands and plopped them in a precarious pile on a white serving plate.

As she selected another loaf to slice, Elsa began to hum a tune with snatches of words that Gennie did not recognize. That in itself wasn't surprising. Over the years, the Shakers had written thousands of songs, and Gennie certainly didn't know all of them. But that Elsa, still a new sister, should know a song that Gennie had never heard, that was surprising.

Gennie paused as she filled another tureen with soup from the large kettle on the stove. Her back was to Elsa, but she knew that voice. Elsa's singing voice was strong and clear and betrayed none of the roughness of her speech. Gennie strained to hear the lyrics. Two lines appeared to be a refrain, repeated between verses. *Mother Ann, Mother Lucy, you speak and I hear; Mother Ann, Mother Lucy, your message is clear.* Not very inventive, Gennie thought as she turned to place her tureen on the table.

Charity's hand shook as she held her butter knife in midair. "What is that song? Where did you learn it?"

Elsa grinned. "At a place thee'll never go to."

"Where? Tell me this instant."

"Everyone will know soon enough," Elsa said, barely above a whisper.

Rose knew that she would have only a few minutes with Molly before the sheriff and Grady would expect to continue their questioning. The two men now stood with the brethren, ready to file out of the east doorway of the dining room.

Grasping the girl firmly by the upper arm, Rose swept her out of the line of sisters exiting the west doorway. Surprised, Molly did not resist, but followed Rose through the kitchen door and over to the far corner behind a large arch kettle. The spicy, comfortable smell of mincemeat still clung to its cast-iron sides.

"Molly, we must be quick," Rose said in an urgent whisper. "You *must* tell me the nature of your relationship with Johann and why you were arguing with him. The sheriff was telling the truth. You were indeed seen arguing with him, and your denial only makes the sheriff suspicious of you. Do you understand?"

Rose knew that if she did not protect Molly, no one else would. The girl was not a sister and, as she herself had said, not likely to become one. Many Believers saw her as hopeless, dishonest, and defiant. Everyone expected her to leave the community, and probably to take to the streets, as soon as she turned eighteen. It would be easier for all of them if a non-Believer were arrested for the killing, even one partly brought up by the Shakers. But Rose could not give up on her. She saw only a frightened seventeen-year-old not bright enough to handle her beauty, not nearly as blasé as she pretended.

Her eyes black with fear, Molly nodded and bit her lower lip. "OK," she said. "I'll tell you. But you'll be mad."

"Just *tell* me."

Molly drew a tremulous breath. She fidgeted with her neckerchief. "Johann and me, we was . . . well, you know, lovers." Molly tilted her chin defiantly. "I loved him, and he loved me, too, no matter what anyone told you. He loved me true."

Rose spent precious moments calming herself. "Are you telling me," she said, "that you and Johann . . . that you fornicated?"

"I reckon that's what you call it. I call it love. You wouldn't understand. You gonna kick me out?"

A sense of failure weighed on Rose's heart. She had thought so much about how to protect Gennie, her favorite, that she had let Molly slip through her fingers.

"Nay, child, I will not ask you to leave. Not now, anyway. But your future depends on you," Rose said.

"Do you have to tell the sheriff what we done?"

Rose was saved from answering immediately as Elsa clumped through the door and clattered her hefty tray on the large oak worktable, followed more quietly by Gennie. Elsa glared at them, distrust tightening her plain features, and swung out again.

Gennie grinned at Molly, and Molly's mouth curved slowly in return. The effect was lovely, turning her eyes a luminous blue-black. Rose was familiar with the cleansing of confession and thought perhaps it was the emotional release that allowed those dark features to soften. That, and friendship. Maybe she and Gennie together could help bring out the good in this sad, rebellious girl.

But time was very short. "You still haven't told me what you argued with Johann about," she said.

Hurt feelings pinched Molly's face into a pout. "He said he didn't want me no more. Said I was just a kid and he wanted someone more growed-up, a 'challenge,' he said."

Molly had been with them for three years, yet they

had taught her so little. She had never learned to value herself as a creature of God. She knew only how to give a man anything he wanted.

"Molly, I believe you have been honest with me. Now I must ask you a difficult question. Look at me and tell me truly, did you kill Johann Fredericks?"

"Nay! I told you, I loved him. Maybe I wanted to kill Charity and any other girl that looked cross-eyed at him. But I wouldn't of hurt Johann. Do you believe me?" Molly sniffled and rubbed a sleeve across her eyelids.

"Yea, I do."

Rose knew that she had to work fast. Sheriff Brock was looking for a reasonable suspect, and he was becoming very suspicious of Molly Ferguson. And the foolish girl had made the situation worse by her behavior.

Gennie returned to the kitchen, alone this time, and Rose gestured urgently for her to join them. Sliding her laden tray onto the cluttered table, Gennie ran to them. With an arm around each girl and a glance toward the dining room, Rose led the group through the outside door.

"Stay in your room, both of you, until I come to fetch you. Don't venture out until then," she warned, "even if it's nearly suppertime. I'll explain to the sisters that you won't be back to work until later. Go now, and stay to the backs of the buildings, but walk at a normal pace." She knew that from a distance the girls would look like any two Shaker sisters.

Rose smoothed a few stray wisps of pale red hair back under her bonnet, squared her shoulders, and walked toward the Trustees' Office, where she had promised to meet Brock and Grady to complete the interview with Molly. She told herself that she would not lie. She would certainly tell the sheriff all that she knew of Molly's tryst. If he asked.

* * *

"Whaddya mean I can't question her no more? She got something to hide?" Sheriff Brock's wiry body was rigid with anger.

"I'm sorry, Sheriff, but I cannot allow her to be upset further. It's my decision, not hers. Molly's mother placed her in our care; she is our responsibility. Perhaps later we can speak to her again."

To her surprise, Brock relaxed. "All right, then," he said, too politely for Rose's comfort. "Grady, what's that other name we got?"

"Preston, Albert Preston."

"Yeah, that's the one. You see, Miss Callahan, we stayed quiet at lunch, like you asked, but afterward, being policemen, we couldn't help but ask a question or two. Seems this Preston also argued with the deceased. So tell us about him."

There were times, Rose thought, when she regretted the famous Shaker honesty. Naturally, the brethren would answer truthfully any questions the sheriff put to them. But it made her task harder when the police riled everyone up before she could talk to them.

"Albert is our carpenter," she admitted. "He is new to this area and has not yet signed the covenant to become one of the brethren, but his novitiate period is nearly finished."

"This Preston's from out of town, you say? Any idea where he's from?"

"I hold few personal conversations with the brethren, Sheriff."

By now Rose knew how Brock thought about this murder. Surely he was thinking that if Albert is a stranger, maybe not even a Kentuckian, he'd make a good suspect. Well, at least Brock had forgotten Molly for the moment.

Feeling tired, Rose led the sheriff and Grady toward the Carpenters' Shop, a short walk from the Trustees' Office, across the central pathway. The distance seemed much longer, though, as Rose passed four young men from Languor lounging on the Trustees' Office steps.

"Hey, Harry," one of the men shouted. "You arrested any of these freaks yet?"

Brock responded with a tolerant smile and slapped one of the men on the shoulder as they passed.

The rhythmic sound of hand-sawing and the crisp smell of freshly cut wood drifted from the open windows of the Carpenters' Shop as Rose escorted the men up the two steps leading to the front door. She pulled the old wooden door and noticed how it swung easily and silently on its hinges. Albert Preston was truly a godsend for the Society. The Carpenters' Shop had been locked and empty for ten years when Albert had arrived and put the old tools to expert use. He had moved a bed to the upstairs room at the back of the building, rather than live in the nearly empty Novitiates' Dwelling House, and he seemed to work around the clock. He was a reserved man, who rarely spoke to anyone. But his carpentry skills were superb. He took to making Shaker oval boxes right away, almost as if he already knew how, and he soon moved on to ladder-back chairs and a beautiful new maple trestle table for the Ministry dining room. If his output continued at this rate, the Society would soon have extra furniture to offer for sale to the world. When not in the Carpenters' Shop, Albert carried his tools from building to building, planing swollen drawers, fixing handles, lovingly smoothing distressed wood wherever he found it. A grateful community was more than ready to accept him as one of them.

Albert raised his eyes briefly as they entered the shop and lowered them again to his task. With a quick, sure movement, he hammered a small, copper tack into the narrow end of one swallowtail in the finger-shaped joint holding together an oval box. Albert smoothed his long fingers over the tack and examined the thin, curved maple from several angles. He seemed satisfied and looked up at the visitors.

"Albert Preston?" Brock asked in a clipped voice.

Albert nodded once.

"Sheriff Harry Brock. Got some questions for you."

Albert was a slight man, shorter than the sheriff, with a gaunt face and deep-set eyes. Rose wondered if he had managed to put on any weight at all since he had arrived, emaciated and coughing, six months earlier. At least the cough had disappeared.

"Where you from, Preston?" Brock asked.

"Back East."

"Where back East?"

"All around. Wandered a lot." Albert still held the oval box and gently rubbed his thumb over its smooth curves.

"Where was you born?"

"Don't remember."

Rose and Grady seemed to be the only ones who saw any humor in this response. Both smiled and caught each other at it.

"We can find out, you know."

"Probably won't be any records. I was an orphan. Folks took me in and sent me to school here and there. Don't remember my parents. Don't even know exactly how old I am."

It was the longest string of words Rose had ever heard Albert utter, and she noted that his speech was educated, and the vowels had an elongated quality that sounded familiar to her.

"Albert," Rose said, "tell us what you know about Johann Fredericks."

He shrugged, calling attention to his work jacket, which hung too loosely from his shoulders. Was the man still ill and not telling them? Rose thought about calling in the doctor from Languor to look at him. Albert would never be the most beloved of the brethren, but he was one of them.

"Didn't know him," Albert said. "Not really, just to talk to in passing. We weren't friends. He wasn't one of the brethren."

"Even so," she continued, "you must have formed some opinions."

"He wasn't much," Albert said.

"What do you mean by that?" Brock demanded.

Albert studied the oval box he still held as though he would find the answer there.

"Winter Shaker," he said. "Only wanted to use us."

Rose nodded, and Brock cocked his head to one side.

"I thought y'all believed in feeding anyone who's hungry," Brock said. "That's sort of askin' to be used, ain't it?"

Albert said nothing. He stroked his thumb against his box as if it were the soft fur of a kitten.

"Where was you a week ago last Thursday, at nine in the evenin' or thereabouts?" Brock asked.

"Union Meeting."

"And after the meetin'?"

"Came back here. Worked a while and went to bed." Albert jerked his head upward to his living quarters upstairs.

"Any witnesses?"

"Nay."

"What about the next Monday night and the morning when the body was found?"

"Here. Alone. As usual."

Brock didn't seem to have much else to ask. Like everyone else, Albert had no alibis. The sheriff nodded at Grady to indicate the interview was at an end, and Grady flipped his notebook shut. Rose allowed herself a relieved sigh. Brock had found no one to arrest yet.

THIRTEEN

AFTER WATCHING SHERIFF BROCK AND GRADY DRIVE off without a suspect in custody, Rose set off to continue her own questioning. She heard the tolling of the Meetinghouse bell and quickened her pace. Four-forty-five already. She would have only a short time before evening meal, and she had two stops to make first.

The Infirmary, conveniently situated in the middle of North Homage, contained a dozen sickrooms and an office. At one time the Society had its own doctor, one of the brethren, but now one sister with nurse's training cared for the sick and called in the physician from Languor when necessary.

Only one sickroom was occupied, and Rose felt a stab of guilt for hurrying past without visiting the elderly sister who slept fitfully in a cradle bed. She would return soon, she promised herself. She would bring a bouquet of lavender and lemon balm to sweeten the air.

Sister Josie, approaching eighty herself, sat behind a desk in her small office, scribbling in a ledger. Her several chins jiggled as she looked up at Rose over a row of glass apothecary jars lined up before her. Her round, pink cheeks gathered in bunches as she smiled.

"Rose, my dear child, I was just thinking of you. I've

been taking inventory of our herbs and thinking I must ask you to raid the Herb House for me!" Her plump arms opened wide as though welcoming a miracle. "But do sit, child, and tell me what your trouble is. Is it illness that makes you look so pale and tired?" She bounced to her feet and pushed Rose into a chair. "Let me get a tonic for you. We must toughen you up for the winter. Nay, sit quiet now," she said, as Rose tried to rise.

"Josie, I am quite well," Rose protested. But Josie flung open a glass-doored medicine cabinet filled with more apothecary jars and tins of various sizes. Humming a lively dance tune, she pulled down several bottles and gathered them in one arm.

"Josie, I'm fine," Rose said. "I've just come to—"

"A moment, child, I must think what is the best formula to help you. Let's see, gentian to stimulate the appetite. It's so bitter, we'll add some peppermint. Then chamomile and valerian, I think, to calm you and help you sleep. Any stomach complaints?" Josie asked without turning.

"Nay, Josie, no stomach complaints, no complaints whatsoever, I just want—"

"Fine, then, this'll do. Won't be a minute, Rose, just sit still and rest. I'll make up a mixture for tea. We'll have you right in no time." She bore her selections back to the desk and lined them up next to a scale, where she measured the portions precisely, squinting down through her reading glasses at the numbers on the dial. Rose bit her lip, fretting about the passing time as Josie mixed the ingredients, ground them in a mortar and pestle, then spooned them into two tins.

"There!" Josie said with her pink smile. "One cup of the gentian and peppermint before each meal and one of chamomile and valerian at bedtime." She plunked the tins in front of Rose and settled back in her chair. "Now, what else can I do for you?"

"Albert Preston. He looks unwell to me. Have you or the doctor seen him lately?"

"Ah, Albert." Josie plunked her chins on her fist and puckered her face in concentration. "Nay, I've not seen him here lately," she said. "I saw him last night, I believe, at supper, and I must say that his color was good. His cough hasn't returned, I'd certainly have noticed that."

"When he came to us last spring, he had a wound, did he not?"

Josie sucked in her lower lip and frowned.

"I know it isn't right to pry," Rose continued, "but Agatha has asked me to look into the death of Johann Fredericks, and I must ask uncomfortable questions."

Josie shook her head sadly. "Poor boy. To die so young, and not yet a full Believer."

Rose thought it best not to discuss the "poor boy's" all-too-worldly activities before his death.

Josie came to her decision with a sprightly nod. "All right, then, if it will help you solve this terrible killing. Albert did indeed come to us very ill, with a festering wound in his thigh. He said he got it when he was attacked as he rode the rails to our doorstep. But I don't see—"

"Is he completely recovered?" Rose wanted to avoid discussing her speculations with anyone but Agatha.

"Yea, for many months."

"You see, he still looks as though he is losing weight. And I know that you always notice if Believers look ill."

Josie pushed out her lips and shook her head slowly. Then her expression cleared. "Ah!" she said, bouncing up in her chair and sending her chins into vibration. "Now I see what concerns you. But his weight has stabilized, I do assure you, it is only that his clothes do not fit. I did take note of that. So," she said, and slapped a palm on her desk. "No need to worry. It's a problem for the tailor, nothing more." Her cheeks piled up again in a grin.

Rose smiled, too. She had the information she needed.

"I'm so relieved," she said.

With less than an hour until the evening meal, Rose scooped up her skirts and trotted the short distance to the Laundry, next door to the Infirmary. The washing machines were quiet and the first floor empty as she entered. The sisters would all be upstairs finishing the drying and ironing before they closed the shop for the day.

She went upstairs and directly to Sister Gretchen, an energetic young woman recently appointed laundry deaconess. Gretchen raised questioning eyebrows at Rose and continued to iron the butternut brown Sabbathday dress draped over her board. Rose explained what she wanted to know as Gretchen's hands smoothed apart gathers in the skirt and pressed away the wrinkles. When Rose had finished, Gretchen paused with her iron inches above the fabric and cocked her head to one side.

"Yea, I do remember now," she said. "However did you guess that, Rose? We noticed that Albert was missing his second set of work clothes, so we sent him a spare to tide him over until the tailor could make him a new set."

"When was this, exactly?"

"Recently, I'm certain. But let me check." Gretchen upended the iron and went to a small desk under a west window. She flipped open a ledger book and ran her finger down a column of dates.

"Ah. Here it is. Just two days ago, on Thursday the twenty-second. Is that all you need to know?"

"Indeed," Rose said. "Indeed it is."

* * *

Sawing sounds through the open window told Rose that Albert was still busy in the Carpenters' Shop, despite the closeness of the dinner hour. He neither heard nor saw her enter, so engrossed was he in cutting a smooth swath through a long piece of maple. Rose watched him in profile, searching her memory for anything she had heard about him and his past. She remembered that he had confessed to having been arrested for theft years earlier, but he had been poor and hungry. Since then he had turned himself around, learned a trade. His gifted way with wood ensured that he need never steal again.

She remembered that when he had first arrived, he had applied himself immediately to whatever work he could find to do. Winter Shakers often vowed that their fervent wish was to sign the covenant as soon as possible to secure a steady place for themselves at the dinner table, but many avoided work.

Since the Society had done little proselytizing recently, anyone who stayed the course and became a novitiate usually either had been brought up by the Shakers or knew of them and sought them out. But Albert seemed to drift in from nowhere. As his health improved, he began asking theological questions, and one day Brother Hugo found him repairing a wobbly bench in the dining room. Hugo, nearing ninety and growing blind, happily turned over to Albert his repair duties and the long unused key to the Carpenters' Shop.

At that moment, Albert glanced up and started when he saw Rose watching him.

"I'm sorry, Albert, but you were so attentive to your work. I didn't wish to distract you. Might I ask you a question or two?"

With clear reluctance, Albert placed his saw on the workbench and slid onto his stool. He nodded.

"I won't keep you, I know you'll want to tidy up the

shop before evening meal, but I'd like to know more about your relationship with Johann Fredericks."

"Told you. Didn't know him."

"But I think you must have. Or at least you know more about his death than you are saying."

Albert's thumb rubbed rhythmically against his finger, while his slight shoulders hunched inside his roomy work shirt. He knew something, she was convinced of that.

"Albert, have you placed an order with the tailor for a new set of work clothes?"

Albert stiffened and narrowed his eyes. "Why?"

"Well, you've lost a set, haven't you? Gretchen noticed when she sorted out your laundry, and she sent you a spare set. That's what you are wearing, isn't it? One can see that it's made for a stockier man."

Albert slid off his stool and turned to his workbench. His back to Rose, he began to tidy up the tools.

"Suits me fine," he said. "Comfortable."

"How did you lose the old set?"

Albert shrugged one shoulder. "Don't know."

"At the time, none of us thought to tell the sheriff to check inside the clothes that Johann wore when Gennie found him. As they are Shaker clothes, he should find the owner's initials sewn inside. Shall I call him now?"

Albert's hand closed around a hammer on the workbench. He held it a few seconds too long before lifting it to a peg. But when he pivoted to face Rose, his face held fear, not threat.

"Those were your clothes, weren't they, on Johann's body?" she continued more gently. "They were Shaker work clothes, too short for him, and your work clothes are missing. It makes sense."

Albert studied his sinewy hands. "My clothes were stolen," he said. "About a week ago. Spilled a bucket of water on them." He waved a hand in the direction of a large bucket in which strips of maple soaked prior to being curved into oval boxes. "So I changed into my spare work clothes and hung the wet ones out in back to dry. Forgot about them till next morning. Came out to fetch them first thing, but they were gone."

"Gone! We've never lost old-style Shaker clothes off a line, even when we hung them outdoors and had visitors all day long. It's hard to believe!"

Albert's face reddened. "Look, I'm telling the truth. I didn't want to say anything because . . . well, because of my past."

"Albert, no one is accusing you of anything. Your past has been forgiven. But it would help me to know who might have stolen those clothes."

"It's clear who stole them, least to me." Albert turned back to his workbench and straightened the last few tools with slow movements.

"Who, then?"

"Whoever killed Johann, of course," he said. "Stands to reason."

FOURTEEN

WITH A BURST OF ENERGY BROUGHT ON BY DELIGHT that her kitchen duty was almost done, Gennie hooked the last of the clean copper pots on their wall pegs.

"You're trottin' like a horse headin' for the barn," Elsa said. "'Course, you didn't work as long as we did."

Not even Elsa's barbs could ruin Gennie's mood. Monday she would be in the Herb House, crumbling those heady fragrances; packing them into round, tin boxes for sale; toting up the day's work and recording the number in the daily journal. Everything she loved most to do in the whole world.

It helped, too, that she'd had a load lifted from her shoulders when Rose got Molly to confess her meeting with Johann. Rose was so clever, Gennie thought, to get Molly to tell. Of course, during their enforced stay in their room that afternoon, Molly had been vague about whether she had told Rose everything, like where she got the nail polish and lipstick and perfume that she kept under her mattress. Even Gennie didn't know that for sure. Well, Rose would figure it out. But just to be sure, Gennie decided she would try to get Molly to confide in her as soon as she got back to their retiring room.

"Charity, may I be excused now?"

Behind her, Elsa scraped a bucket across the floor. "Nay," Elsa said loudly, "there's no call for y'all to be runnin' off when we still got work to do. Git thyself over here and mop this floor." She held out her dripping mop.

Gennie hesitated and watched Charity, whose pinched face flushed with anger. "Elsa, just because your own work is not completed does not mean that Eugenie should do it for you. Yea, of course, Eugenie, run along," Charity said, as Gennie had hoped she would as soon as Elsa challenged her authority as kitchen deaconess.

Gennie smiled her thanks and hurried through the outside door so that she would not have to pass close to Elsa. She was glad to get away from both women and their perpetual bickering.

At 9:00 P.M. it had long been dark, and a damp wind penetrated the thin fabric of Gennie's dress. The afternoon had warmed up enough that when Rose came to fetch them, after the sheriff left, she and Molly had hurried back to work without their cloaks. Gennie raced toward the Children's Dwelling House, hoping that Molly had stoked up the stove in their room. Knowing Molly, she wouldn't be asleep yet. She would probably be combing her luxurious hair or fussing with her secret hoard of makeup. Gennie hoped so; it would give her an opening to try once more to find out where the items came from.

To warm her blood, Gennie sprinted up the Dwelling House steps and the inner staircase. She arrived panting at the door of her retiring room and pushed it open after a perfunctory knock. The room was dark. Through the uncovered windows the moonlight outlined the shapes of furniture, including Molly's neatly made bed. The cold stove and open window shades indicated that Molly had not been back since before sunset. Her work in the Laundry would have ended in time for the evening meal. Her cloak was missing from its peg, so she must have come back just before or after her meal to fetch it. Maybe Elder Wilhelm had given her evening duty harvesting apples. Everyone had to pitch in right now. That must be it.

Gennie lit a lamp, drew the shades, and started a fire in the woodstove. She kept it small, since she would be in bed soon. She pulled her nightdress from a drawer built into the wall, laid it on her bed, and pulled off her shoes. But something kept her from undressing. Gennie was rarely alone in this room. It was deadly quiet. She tucked her feet underneath her on her own bed and stared at Molly's empty one. A slight bulge on the far edge, probably invisible if she hadn't known what was there, betrayed Molly's cache of beauty items.

Without stopping to think, Gennie slipped across the room and slid her hand under Molly's mattress. Her fingers closed around a small, oblong object, probably the Ruby lipstick. She drew it out and pulled off the lid. It was a different shade, more pink than red. Pretty Pink, it said on the bottom. The stick was perfect, unused.

Beyond her door, Gennie heard quick footsteps and a girl's laughter. With shaking hands, she crammed the top back on the lipstick, nicking the pink smoothness. Molly would know that someone had been looking at her things. Well, too late to worry about that now. Gennie slid the lipstick back under the mattress, wishing she had been more careful to remember exactly where she'd found it. She dashed to the stove and stoked it, waiting for her breath to come more evenly.

The footsteps passed her door and went on down the hall. Her heart still thumping, Gennie shoved the poker into the fire and raced to her own bed. Her quick, shallow breathing made her feel light-headed.

This is wrong, she thought. *I shouldn't be digging through Molly's things.*

Gennie forced herself to take deep breaths. Her heartbeats gradually slowed to a more normal pace. She glanced again at Molly's bed. Maybe it wasn't right, but she had to know if there was anything else that Molly hadn't shown her. The pink lipstick was brand-new. Was Molly still receiving gifts? If so, then they were not coming from Johann. Was she seeing another man?

This time she poked her head out the door and listened for footsteps on the stairs. The lamps cast shadows in the deserted corridors. She had never before noticed how silent the building could be at night.

She eased the door shut and raced to Molly's bed before her courage evaporated. Grasping the edges of the thin mattress with both hands, she lifted it from the pad underneath. Along the outer edge, arranged in a crooked row, were five items: red nail polish, the mother-of-pearl-handled nail file, two lipsticks, and a small bottle made of pale blue glass. Balancing the mattress on one elbow, Gennie lifted the glass bottle. Lavender Eau de Toilette, it said on the front. She sniffed the cap. The cloying sweetness smelled nothing like the fresh scent of the lavender buds drying in the Herb House. The Shakers distilled rose petals into rosewater for cooking, but somehow it still smelled like roses when it was done. Why ruin a scent, Gennie wondered, when the original was so perfect?

She carefully replaced the bottle as she had found it, label down, and rearranged the lipstick she had shoved back so hurriedly. She lowered the mattress to the bed and smoothed the bedclothes.

In the distance, the bell over the Meetinghouse rang the hour. Ten o'clock. Normally they would be drifting off to an exhausted sleep by now, after such a long day. Where could Molly be?

Still dressed, Gennie stretched out on her own bed and pulled her coverlet up to her chin. Maybe Molly had sneaked out for a walk. It was the sort of thing she would do, though never this late before and not on such a chilly night.

Molly loved to visit the quiet Shaker cemetery, now unused, on the edge of North Homage. The graves were old, all but a few with simple, deteriorating markers bearing only the initials of the deceased. None was more recent than the end of the last century, when a new cemetery had been created on the other side of the village. The old cemetery was usually deserted and, because of its location at the edge of a drop-off, it provided a panoramic view of the surrounding land. Gennie had found her roommate there more than once, sitting with her back to a small tombstone, watching the movements on the farms nearby. It gave Gennie the shivers. Molly was actually sitting on the grave of an eldress, but that didn't seem to bother her. It was the best place to watch the world outside their little village. But surely Molly wouldn't go there at such a late hour, would she?

Under the warmth of the coverlet, Gennie's body relaxed, and her eyes closed. Her shoulders ached from the hours of rolling pie crusts. How many pies had they made? Charity would have kept count and recorded the number in her journal. Gennie knew she could ask the next day, if she cared to know, but she didn't. Pies were not nearly so interesting to count as tins of dill and marjoram and thyme. And lavender and rosemary. Gennie drifted to sleep with the comforting names floating across the backs of her eyelids.

She slept in a field of lavender, the intensely fragrant buds just beginning to open. She looked up at a peaceful sky through dense purple stems swaying above her head, but as she reached up to touch one it turned wet and sticky. And then the thick liquid engulfed her, pinning her to the bottom of a lavender lake. She struggled upward. As she reached toward the light, a vibration rocked her slowly back and forth as if she were trapped in a vat of thickening jelly. A body floated past her, rocking downward. The still body of a girl wrapped in a dark cloak, her long, black hair billowing around her head in thick tendrils. Gennie thrashed her arms and legs, unable to save the girl or herself.

With a strangled cry, she sat up in bed, her eyes open but unseeing. Her breath came in panting whimpers. She had left the lamp lit, and as her eyes focused she saw Molly's still-empty bed and her own coverlet crumpled on the floor, where she had tossed it.

The half hour chimed. How long had she slept? Gennie pushed aside an edge of the window shade and surveyed the darkened community. She saw no lights in the south side of the Trustees' Office. Could it be 11:30 or even later?

Gennie had to look for Molly. Maybe it was just the aftereffects of the lavender-sea dream, but she feared her roommate was in danger. She thought about going to Rose. It would be so much easier and less frightening. But if Molly had met with a man, Gennie would get her into terrible trouble.

To be honest, Gennie was afraid to tell Rose about her dream. Everybody argued these days about dreams, with Elder Wilhelm encouraging visions and Elsa doing spirit drawings from designs she said appeared to her in dreams. Rose agreed with Eldress Agatha that such things were all right a hundred years ago, when the rest of America was holding séances and having their palms read, but not now. Gennie feared Rose would think her under Wilhelm's influence.

Gennie slipped into her heaviest shoes and her long wool cape. She left her bonnet hanging on its peg. Too much trouble. Everyone would be in bed; no one would know she'd left her hair uncovered. Easing the door closed behind her, she crept down the staircase, keeping close to the wall, where fewer boards creaked.

Outside, the crisp, still air shocked her to alertness. Bright moonlight caressed the silent village, illuminating the neatly trimmed walkways and the spare simplicity of the buildings. Gennie dashed across the central path and through the dew-damp grass toward the cemetery. She drew her hood close to her head to avoid seeing the dark, eerie corners which the moonlight couldn't penetrate.

The old cemetery had been used when North Homage was small and young and gave little thought to whether they had enough burial space. The spot had spiritual meaning. Their first eldress had a vision very near the drop-off marking the western edge, where she had stood to relay messages from long-dead Believers. In a more practical vein, the early Believers were afraid that their cattle would graze too close to the edge of the drop-off and slide down. So the spot became a cemetery.

For the safety of the living, the brethren had stretched a three-slatted fence across the edge of the drop-off. On the other three sides, they had built thick fieldstone fences by piling large, flat pieces of Kentucky limestone horizontally in a jigsaw pattern, topped off with a row of additional flat pieces balanced side by side vertically. A wooden gate provided the only entrance.

To Gennie that night, the fieldstone fence looked like a massive, open jaw, lined with jagged teeth. She felt a prick of fear as she peered over the fence's saw-toothed top. It reached just above her waist, and it felt like a shield between her and the dim shapes on the other side.

"Molly, are you here?" she called softly, then "Molly," again, with more force. Silence.

This is foolish, she thought. *I know Rose would say*

so. Fear turned to anger with Molly, the reason she was out here feeling cold and silly and a little bit frightened. She shivered, pulled her cape tight, and followed the wall until she came to the entryway. The wooden gate felt cold and slippery. It screeched as she inched it inward.

As if in response, a cry of pain, faint but clear, pierced the still, night air. Gennie froze. It seemed to come from behind her. Sound travels far at night, she knew. She strained to hear above the thudding of her own heart, but she heard nothing more. Propelled by growing alarm, Gennie hurried around the inside perimeter of the cemetery, squinting at the crooked markers.

The Shakers' humility was reflected in their choice of small, metal markers, most inscribed only with initials and birth and death dates. But one especially beloved eldress rested under a larger, well-worn marble plaque, which faced toward Languor and was broad enough to hide a girl sitting in front of it. Gennie peered around the gravestone. The moon floated behind a cloud and left the cemetery in near darkness. She could still make out shapes, though, and none looked like Molly.

She was halfway around, intent only on finishing and racing to her room, when she heard the sound of creaking hinges. She froze and squinted into the darkness covering the silent grave markers, toward the gate. Framed in the opening was a huge figure, bearlike in size, with a large furry head and powerful shoulders. It stepped inside the gate. Thick arms swung at its side as it took another step, then a third, straight across the graves and toward her.

She spun around, desperate for an escape. She couldn't reach the gate without passing the creature, nor could she take her chances leaping over the slatted fence to the drop-off before he—or it—could stop her. She tossed her cape back to free her arms and clutched at the rough fieldstone fence beside her. The stone edges felt sharp enough to pierce her palms.

"Halt there!" said an angry voice in a hoarse whisper.

Gennie whipped around to see the creature lumber toward her, his face still hidden by shadow. Was this what Johann had seen just before he died? She tried to mumble a prayer, but none came to her.

Scooping up her heavy skirt with one hand, she flung herself at the fieldstone fence. She poked frantically at the horizontal layers with her foot. After several agonized moments, she found a foothold and dragged one leg over the serrated rim of the fence, terror numbing her skin to the pain as the rock scraped through her stocking.

"Who is that? This is desecration! Halt now!" The voice, resonant with outrage, boomed close behind her. Gennie paused, straddling the fence. She had heard that deep timbre before—preaching at Sunday worship service.

Elder Wilhelm grabbed her around the waist and yanked her back into the cemetery grounds. She yelped as a razor-sharp stone scraped the inside of her thigh. He twirled her around to face him.

"Eugenie!" He dropped his hands from her waist and leaped back. "Is no one in bed tonight? Thy bonnet. Where is thy bonnet?" Gennie understood. Had he seen the outline of her bonnet, he would not have touched her as he did.

The returning moonlight lit his features. His lower eyelids drooped as though he hadn't been sleeping well, and his eyes were feverishly bright. Gennie wondered if he were ill or just very angry, but when he spoke again, his voice sounded tired, even defeated.

"Child," he said, "it is not safe to be out alone at night. I'll not ask thy reasons for being here, they must be shared with the eldress in confession. Go back now to thy retiring room and to bed." He stepped aside and waved her past. Her trembling legs wouldn't budge.

"Run now, run along," he said, with more of his old impatience.

With fumbling fingers, she gathered up her cape and skirts and flew through the dark until she saw the silhouette of the Children's Dwelling House. Once inside the building, her fear-induced energy drained away. Gasping, she used the railing to pull herself up the stairs, no longer caring if anyone heard her. Without knocking, she slipped into her darkened retiring room.

Too tired to undress, she stumbled toward her bed. Even in the dark, she knew her way. With a sigh that was half moan, she slid between the sheets and pulled the coverlet over her head for comfort. She had no strength left for thought or worry about Molly, and even the throbbing scrape on her thigh could not keep her awake.

She began to sink into a dreamless sleep, when a strong arm grasped her shoulder.

"Gennie Malone, it's past midnight!" Molly's voice sounded hoarse through the layers of fabric. Gennie snapped awake as her coverlet was flung aside.

"Where you *been?*"

FIFTEEN

"WHERE HAVE *I* BEEN?! MOLLY FERGUSON, I OUGHT to . . . to . . ." Gennie was so angry she couldn't think of a painful enough punishment for her roommate. She swung herself to her feet. Both girls stood with their arms akimbo, glaring at each other in the dark. "Do you have any idea what I went through tonight to find you? You were gone *forever* and I thought something awful had happened to you. Where *were* you?"

"I can take care of myself," Molly whispered harshly. "You're the one oughta be horsewhipped. I been worried sick about you."

"You? You probably were sound asleep when I came in," Gennie said.

"Was not."

"You were, too. Now you're just trying to keep me from asking where you were. You'd better tell me this minute, Molly Ferguson, or I'll march right out in the hall and call over to the Trustees' Office, and I'll tell Rose everything, and I'll tell it loudly, too, so everybody in the House can hear." Gennie crossed her arms and flopped on her bed.

"Yell a little louder, most everybody can hear you now," Molly said. She grabbed a corner of Gennie's coverlet and pulled it over her shoulders as she, too, plunked down on the bed. "Look, I wasn't nowhere,

OK? I was just walkin'. I like to get out, you know that."

"I went to the cemetery. You weren't there," Gennie said.

"The cemetery? Did you go anywhere else?" Molly sounded startled, but her eyes were dark hollows, unreadable in the dim light.

Gennie thought she saw something else, too. She switched on her bedside light. She was right, one eye was darker than the other. The skin around Molly's left eye was swollen and red.

"Molly, what happened? Who hurt you?"

"Nobody. It's none of your business. Leave me alone." Molly jumped to her feet and flipped off Gennie's light.

Gennie heard her crawl back into her own bed.

"Are you going to tell me where you were?"

"Ain't nothin' to tell," Molly whispered.

Rose awakened making lists in her head. It was Sunday, a bright and glorious morning, and she had preparations to make, tasks to complete, and many questions to ask. First priority, the worship service. It was now too late to cancel the public portion of the service, so she would take what precautions she could to control the crowds. She had Agatha's permission to limit the number of people in the Meetinghouse and to keep the small children away from the service.

She tossed off her covers and dressed quickly, then straightened her room with frenzied speed. The bell rang five times, still an hour before Sabbathday breakfast, so she went downstairs to her office to pull the lists from her head and write them down.

By 5:45, she had filled a sheet of paper. She picked up her phone and made an indecently early call to Deputy Grady O'Neal, who clearly had been asleep.

"Uh, Rose?" He responded groggily. "Is anything wrong? Is Gennie all right?"

Rose hesitated. She feared bringing Grady and Gennie together. She could lose Gennie, and that would cause her pain. She wasn't sure she trusted either Grady or Brock. Neither had a good reason to help the Shakers. She remembered the quickly hidden hatred on Grady's face when he examined Johann's body. Her knowledge of Grady was too sketchy. But to trust no police might put Gennie's life—and the lives of others—in great danger.

"All is well so far, Grady," she said. "But I do need your help. Are you on duty today?"

"Nope, free as a bird."

"Good. Then would you come to our worship service this afternoon? It begins at 1:00 P.M., but you might come early. Have a light midday meal with us. And do not wear your uniform." She preferred that Wilhelm not know that she had taken matters into her own hands.

That task accomplished, Rose glanced at the office clock. Time to gather for breakfast. She threw her cloak over her shoulders and cut across the grass between the Trustees' Office and the dining room next door. Halfway there, she saw Sheriff Brock walk briskly away from the Children's Dwelling House. He didn't see her.

What was he doing near the Children's House? Should she rush after him and demand to know? The bell tolled. Breakfast was starting, and maybe he hadn't been at the dwelling house, after all. She let him go.

Rather than line up at the dining room's west doorway with the other sisters, she went directly to the kitchen door. There would just be time, she thought, to schedule a talk with Elsa for after breakfast. But when she entered the kitchen, she saw only Charity and two young girls, all tearing around the room with trays too full to hold steadily. Rose hung her cloak on a peg and scooped up a tray that was slipping from the grasp of a thirteen-year-old.

"It's for the brethren's table," the girl said, and flew off to fetch another.

Rose carried the steaming bowls of porridge out to the brethren and served them silently. As she did so she scanned the room for Elsa, without success. On her return to the kitchen, she found Charity, her cheeks flushed and oatmeal dribbling down her white neckerchief, filling bowls too quickly and wiping off spills with an apron tied loosely at her waist. Rose found a ladle and began filling bowls from the opposite end of the tray, so that they met in the middle. Only when all the trays were on their way to the dining room did Charity break her concentration. She sagged into a ladder-back chair constructed for a much larger person, so that she looked childlike and overwhelmed.

"It was kind of you to help us," she said. "The girls are too small for such heavy work." She looked as though she were also too slight for such work, but Rose had been impressed by the ease with which she had whisked the laden trays into the dining room. *The Shaker life builds strong young women,* Rose thought with pride.

"Is Elsa ill this morning?" Rose asked. Normally Elsa, with her strong country arms, would have carried the heavier items.

"Nay," Charity said with a sniff. "Elsa was excused from work to pray alone. *Excused,* when there is work to be done! I've never heard of such a thing."

"But surely Agatha did not excuse her," Rose said. "I spoke with her only last night, and she said nothing about it."

"Not Agatha. Wilhelm. He said that the eldress would agree."

"*Would* agree," Rose said. "So in fact he did not ask her." Rose frowned. For Elder Wilhelm to have usurped the eldress's authority with the sisters was serious indeed. The reason must be profoundly important to Wilhelm, and it involved Elsa. Rose added another item to her mental list. She would talk to Agatha, try to get her to confront Wilhelm. She would have to speak with the eldress soon, so that the meeting could occur during the midday meal in the Ministry dining room, when Agatha and Wilhelm would be alone.

"I'll send Gennie and Molly to help you prepare for the midday meal," she said to Charity.

Charity gave a tired smile for thanks and dragged herself from her chair as the remains of breakfast arrived.

Rose turned to leave, then paused. "Charity, do you know where and why Elsa has gone to pray?"

"Nay," Charity said. "Nor do I care. It will take more than a morning of prayer to make her a true Believer."

Eldress Agatha looked ill. Her pallid skin seemed to be melting away, molding itself more each day to the shapes of the frail bones underneath. A hand tremor shook the cup of tea she raised slowly to her lips.

"Do have some of my tea, Rose," she said, in a voice that seemed stronger than her body. "Josie said it was 'strengthening.' And she did mention that you were looking less vigorous than usual, yourself." She smiled thinly, but it was enough to soften her gaunt face.

Rose put her hand over the one that twitched in Agatha's lap.

"Is tea all you've had today? You must try to eat. Josie's tonics are miraculous, but food is more strengthening. Let me fetch you some oatmeal from the kitchen."

"Nonsense, Rose, but don't worry so about me. I no longer work in the fields, I can afford to miss a meal now and then." She withdrew her hand and patted Rose's. "Now," she continued, "tell me why you've come to see me again so soon."

Rose sighed inwardly. Her plan would never work.

Agatha was too ill to confront Wilhelm, and no one else had the authority to do it in her stead. For a moment, Rose, too, felt her strength ebb away. She was losing her mentor, her guardian, her dear, dear friend. Agatha had always been there, calm and quietly powerful, a gentle force.

"It's nothing," Rose said. "I only wanted to see how you are."

Those sunken eyes bored through Rose. "Even during the worst of times," Agatha said sternly, "you never felt it necessary to lie to me. I do not fear death, I welcome it. But not just yet. In the meantime, I expect you to treat me as you always have, with honesty."

Rose smiled. "You have made yourself abundantly clear, my friend," she said. And she told Agatha what she had learned about the killing of Johann Fredericks, the reactions of the suspects, and Wilhelm's control over Elsa.

"Well," said Agatha, when Rose had finished. "I see that we have some work to do. I will speak to Wilhelm during lunch, and you must join us."

"He will interpret my presence as favoritism on your part."

"Perhaps."

"It will only make him more determined to send me away."

"As long as I am alive, you stay here. And after I am gone, I am confident the Lead Ministry will see the wisdom of making you eldress."

All Rose truly wanted was for everything to stay as it was, herself as trustee, not eldress, not gatherer of new souls. She wanted Agatha always to be there. In her own way, she was as loath to change as Wilhelm.

"Are you sure you feel well enough to confront Wilhelm?"

"My dear," Agatha said, smiling gently, "what strength I possess comes from God, and it grows as my body weakens. He has always given me what I needed to do what I must. You will find the same to be true when you are eldress. Now," she said before Rose could respond, "go about your other business. Come collect me at noon. I'll rest until then." She leaned back in her rocking chair and closed her eyes. Rose took the teacup from her lap and placed it on the table next to her, then leaned over to kiss her forehead. Her skin felt cool and smooth and comforting.

"Oh, Rose, *must* I work in the kitchen again? You don't understand how awful it is, with Charity and Elsa fighting all the time." It wasn't like Gennie to pout and whine, but she couldn't help it. It was just too unfair.

"It's only for a day, and Elsa won't be there," Rose said with more sternness than she normally used with Gennie. "And Molly will be with you. Where is Molly, by the way?"

"Um, well, she missed breakfast today. It *is* Sunday, you know, and we weren't supposed to have to work, and anyway Molly says she doesn't need breakfast." She didn't mention that her roommate still slept, exhausted and nursing a swollen eye. She also hadn't told Rose about Molly's stock of beauty items or about her own midnight adventure in the old cemetery. She ought to tell, but Molly made her promise. She said she'd use makeup to cover the bruises and everything would be fine.

"Everyone needs breakfast," Rose said. "And we often have to work on Sunday, young lady, so I don't want to hear any more complaining."

Gennie sighed. "I know, I'm sorry. It's only that I dislike the kitchen, and I always seem to end up there."

"You will be in the Herb House by this time tomorrow!" Rose laughed and hugged Gennie's drooping shoulders. "Maybe I do call on you to help out more than some of the other girls. But it's because I know I can count on you."

Gennie flushed with pleasure, mixed with guilt.

"Run and get that lazy Molly out of bed now," Rose said. "If you work fast, you may both take a break to go to the public worship service, though you will have to slip out early to help Charity prepare the evening meal." She smiled and gave Gennie an affectionate push.

Gennie returned the smile with a feeble one of her own and headed for the Children's Dwelling House, her mind in turmoil. Protecting Molly grew less simple and more costly with each new episode.

"Why does she have to get into so much trouble?" Gennie grumbled to herself.

She stomped up the staircase and burst open the door without knocking, ready to rip the covers off her sleeping roommate. Since all other residents of the house would be at morning worship, she tossed the door shut behind her and enjoyed the bang it made.

The room was empty. Her roommate's bed, where Molly had mumbled that she planned to stay until noon, was neatly made and empty. Her cloak no longer hung on its peg.

"She's gone off *again!*" Gennie said aloud. "Well, I'm not going to look for her, not this time. She can just get into trouble." She turned to leave, then hesitated with her hand on the doorknob. She craned her head around to Molly's bed. It looked as it had the day before, no lumpier, but Gennie ached to take one more peek under the mattress.

Within seconds she had raced to Molly's bed and yanked up the mattress. What she saw brought her to her knees with excitement. Two items had joined the others: a shiny, gold, face-powder compact and an envelope, smudged with dirty stains. Ignoring the compact, she picked up the envelope and turned it over. The gum seal had been broken. With a shaking finger, Gennie lifted the flap and peeked inside. Shaker children had little need for money, but she certainly recognized it when she saw it. A thick wad of it. She pulled the bills out of the envelope and flipped through them. It was all in ones and fives, and there must have been at least $100. She fanned the crisp bills out in her hand, awed by the feel of them. Where would a seventeen-year-old Shaker girl get such a fortune? When a boy or girl decided to leave the Society, the Believers often gave them some money to help them get started, but Molly was still too young for that.

Too late, Gennie heard the door click. She looked over her handful of bills to see Molly framed in the doorway.

"You! You're the one been messin' with my stuff!" She slammed the door behind her.

Gennie lost her balance and slid to the floor, loosening her grip on the money. A clump of green bills fluttered around her, and Molly skidded to her knees to scoop them up.

"Gimme those," she said, and grabbed the batch still clutched in Gennie's hand. Dragging her hand between her mattress and the pad underneath, Molly raked out all her shiny prizes and shoved them, along with the money, into the pockets of her dress.

Gennie jumped to her feet and stood over Molly.

"Where did you get that money? You'd better tell me, I mean it."

"You can't have it, it's mine, and I'm gonna hide it where you ain't never gonna find it. You're supposed to be my friend!"

"I am your friend, and I don't want any of that money," Gennie said with exasperation. "I just want to know what you've gotten yourself into. This isn't right. It isn't right for you to have all these things. And all that money! That's where you were last night, isn't it? You were meeting someone who gave you that money. Is that the person who hit you? *What's going on?*"

"Everyone's against me, even you! I thought you was different, but you're just like all of them. You don't know what it's like to really want things, to want things so bad you dream about them at night, and you feel like you'd do anything for someone who'd get them for you." Molly's dusky eyes flashed with the intensity of her desire and with something more, maybe fear. Her hands clutched at the deep pockets of her work dress, which held the treasures worth so much to her.

"Molly, you're in trouble, aren't you? Let us help you. Rose can. Come on, let's go talk to her." Gennie reached out her hand and touched Molly's sleeve.

Molly yanked her arm back. "You just want my stuff. You and Rose and all of you can just mind your own business." She whirled around and grabbed her heavy cloak off a wall peg. Throwing it around her shoulders, she flew out the door.

"Wait! Molly, please wait!" Gennie raced after her, but Molly's long legs hurtled her down the stairs as fast as they could, her cloak billowing around her. She did not look back. By the time Gennie ran out the front door, she saw Molly round the corner of the building and head toward the Water House.

Charity had the kitchen barely under control when Gennie arrived. The kitchen deaconess had chosen a simple menu of soup and bread, and two young girls flew back and forth through the connecting door to the dining room, carrying crockery and napkins. Judging by the small stature of the girls, Gennie knew she would be carrying the soup tureens. She would have sore arms again by evening. Why did she have to do all the work around here? She tore off her cloak and flung it carelessly on a peg.

"Where's Molly?" Charity asked, looking up from her soup kettle.

Gennie shrugged. If she didn't actually say anything, maybe a shrug wouldn't count as a lie. She walked over and smelled the soup, a spicy cream of squash.

"Taste it for me," Charity said, handing Gennie a

spoon. "I can't seem to taste much these days. Honestly, I don't know what is happening to us lately. Where can Molly be?"

Gennie chose that moment to sip. "More ginger," she said.

"How can I be expected to run the kitchen without adequate help?" Charity complained, reaching for the ginger jar. "Well, I will, that's all. I don't need Elsa."

"What can I do?" Gennie asked.

"Oh, have the girls finished setting the tables? Well, it doesn't matter. Just set up the tureens on the table, then we'll—oh my, is that the brethren arriving? Quickly, carry out the bread. They'll have to cut it themselves. Nay, first move the tureens over here, then deliver the bread."

Gennie arranged the tureens, then grabbed two plates holding loaves of heavy, dark bread and pushed through the door to the dining room, as the sisters and brethren filed silently through their separate doors and seated themselves on benches on opposite sides of the room. On her third trip out, she clattered a plate in front of a young man with straight brown hair, wearing a blue flannel shirt. She steadied the plate, whispering an apology, and looked into the smiling, blue eyes of Grady O'Neal.

"I see no reason why a trustee should be here," Wilhelm said, without looking at Rose. "This is the Ministry dining room. If we must hold a business meeting, we can do so at the Trustees' Office."

"I require her presence, Wilhelm," Eldress Agatha said.

The three Believers grew silent as a young sister brought in a tureen of soup. She placed it near Rose, who filled Agatha's bowl and then her own. Rose watched as Wilhelm ladled the steamy, orange liquid into his bowl. He sat directly across from Agatha at the new trestle table which Albert Preston had created for the two of them. The table was long enough for several additional diners, in case the Society should grow again and have need of a larger Ministry for several separate Shaker families, or groups of Believers living together.

Rose looked around her. The Ministry dining room, a reduced version of the Center Family House dining room, felt cozy and warm. It sparkled from regular cleaning and the bright light from the large windows. Wooden pegs, mostly empty, rimmed the wall, as they did in all other rooms. Wilhelm's straw hat hung on a peg on one side, and Agatha's heavy, outdoor bonnet hung on the other. The eldress rarely used that bonnet anymore.

In this room, the Ministry discussed the spiritual direction of North Homage, unrestricted by the silence and strict separation of the sexes imposed on the larger dining room. Rose had never eaten in the room before, and the significance of her being there now was plain. The ailing Agatha wanted Rose to succeed her as eldress. Torn by conflicting feelings about Agatha's desire, Rose wished the meeting could have taken place in the Trustees' Office. That was her home territory, where she felt in command and at ease. She loved being a trustee, enjoyed watching over the day-to-day existence of her community, keeping the books, doing business with the world. It suited her. If she were eldress, she would feel isolated and more responsible for spiritual decisions that came uneasily to her practical nature. And Wilhelm would be her partner in this enterprise.

"Now then, Wilhelm," Agatha said, when the young sister had withdrawn to the small Ministry kitchen, "I understand that you released Elsa from kitchen duty for an entire morning of solitary prayer." Her voice was firm and strong, and only Rose guessed what the effort must cost her.

Wilhelm broke off a piece of bread and let the crumbs fall into his soup. "And what is thy objection to prayer, eldress?" he asked.

"Work is prayer, too. What kind of prayer is it that requires a sister to leave her work undone?" Agatha snapped. "Worse yet, what kind of sister leaves another to do her work while she wanders off to pray alone?"

"It was necessary."

"The sisters are my concern. I will decide what is necessary for them." Agatha slapped her thin, white hand flat on the table in a gesture of angry authority. The tremor was hardly noticeable. Agatha was drawing upon reserves of strength that would soon be gone.

The expression on Wilhelm's face moved swiftly from surprised to irritated to conciliatory. He carefully placed his utensils on the table and leaned toward the eldress.

"I wish that I could make thee understand," he said. "What I do is for the good of the Society. Agatha, we are dying. Surely I don't need to tell thee how weakened we have become. We have dwindled to only thirty Believers, many growing too old to work." He raked a hand through his thick white hair and slumped back. "What few new Believers join us usually leave within a year or two. Most newcomers are no more than Winter Shakers, at the worst they are liars and fornicators, like that Fredericks man. The few children we bring up leave as soon as they are able. The fire is gone, Agatha, it has gone out, and we must relight it. We *must.* And we can do that only if we withdraw from the world. We must remember who we are, who we were at our strongest." Wilhelm tightened his hand into a fist and held it in the air between himself and the eldress.

"We have discussed this before, Wilhelm," Agatha said. "You know my views. Our strength has always been our adaptability, our ability to accept God's will for us. The world is changing, but it still needs us, I believe that. But the world will only accept our guidance if they respect us. All this traveling back in time to old Shaker dress and speech and ways of behaving, it makes us seem strange, even frightening. I've gone along with it so far because, well, I suppose because it's how I was brought up and part of me yearns to be young again. But I cannot allow you to take charge of the sisters, nay, that is going too far, Wilhelm. Elsa must be returned to my care at once."

Wilhelm smiled. "It is too late."

SIXTEEN

RELEASED FROM KITCHEN DUTY, GENNIE BROKE INTO a skipping run which carried her toward the Meetinghouse, her cloak bouncing around her. The chill of early morning had brightened into a crisp, sunny afternoon.

Gennie felt the sun without seeing it. She was almost sure that Grady would be at the worship service. She raced past the Sisters' Shop and the Infirmary, smiling to herself. She was so distracted by her daydreams that she had nearly reached the Meetinghouse when it struck her that she was passing more and more strangers. She slowed to a walk. It looked and sounded like market day in Languor, with people jostling each other for walking space, horses tied up to any post or bit of fence available. A few cars had pulled onto the lawn near the Meetinghouse, gouging ruts into the lush Kentucky bluegrass. Groups of ten or fifteen, some holding children on their shoulders, clustered around each window, jockeying for the best view.

A sudden prick of fear pushed Gennie through the crowd toward the west doorway, where two sisters tried to convince a group of loud men and women that they would not fit inside. People were packed so tightly in front of the door that Gennie could only stand on her tiptoes and wave at the nearest sister to get her attention. When the sister turned toward her, Gennie recognized Josie, the infirmary nurse, her normally genial face tight with tension. "Look, it's one of them," a male voice close to her said. The voice didn't sound friendly.

"She's just a slip of a girl," said another voice, a woman this time. "Someone oughta take her away from these Shaker people; this ain't no place for a young'un."

Gennie waved frantically and called Josie's name.

"Eugenie! Oh, child, come through quickly," Josie shouted, her eyes wide with alarm. "Move aside now, let the girl through."

Gennie recognized the clipped, firm voice that Josie used with recalcitrant patients who did not respond to gentleness. She had heard that even Elder Wilhelm took his tonic when Josie told him to. It worked here, too. A small crack appeared, through which Gennie could see Josie, small and round and determined, hands on plump hips, facing down a husky man more than a head taller.

"Young man," Josie said, "stand aside this instant. A strapping man like you should be protecting the young ones from this crowd, not making such a fuss all for yourself. Now let the girl through." He shrugged and moved aside. Josie's hand shot out to grab Gennie's and pull her quickly through the door.

"Well, then, that's that!" Josie said with a hint of her normal joviality. "The children's seats have all been grabbed up by those selfish . . . well, just run along and sit with the sisters. Were any more Believers behind you?"

"None that I saw."

"We'll bolt the door, then. That it's come to this . . ."

Gennie made her way to the sisters' benches, choosing a seat near the back. Rows of benches lined both ends of the large meeting room. Visitors filled every inch that wasn't reserved for Believers. They stood around and behind the benches, and even crammed into the deep blueberry-trimmed windowsills. Only the center was empty, the polished pine floor waiting for softly shod dancing feet.

A clear, strong tenor rose above the din and began singing "Simple Gifts," a sweet tune that never failed to please visitors from the world. Many had heard it so often that they knew the words, though they did not understand the meaning.

'Tis the gift to be simple,
'Tis the gift to be free,
'Tis the gift to come down where we ought to be,
And when we find ourselves in the place just right,
'Twill be in the valley of love and delight.

By the end of the short song, the room was quiet. The brother began the tune again, and other Believers—and even some outsiders—joined in, so captivated by the melody that they could put aside fear and anger for the few moments it took to sing it.

When true simplicity is gained,
To bow and to bend, we shan't be ashamed.
To turn, turn, will be our delight
'Til by turning, turning we come round right.

The murmuring began again as the singer fell silent. Three of the sisters, including the one sitting next to Gennie, rose from their seats and moved to stand near the tenor, who had been joined by two more of the brethren to form a chorus.

Gennie glanced at the visitors on the women's side. Most were dressed in their Sunday finery, probably worn earlier to their own church services before they came to North Homage for some free entertainment.

She saw no red dress, but wedged between two plump matrons she found her roommate. Molly craned her neck as though searching for someone on the men's side. She reached up to the strings of her bonnet, gave a tug, and pulled it off. Crushing it under her arm, she slipped off the thin, white cap underneath, then yanked out the pins holding back her hair. Piles of thick, black hair slid to her shoulders. Face powder muted the darkness around her eye.

She's done it this time, Gennie thought, and glanced automatically at the Ministry's observation window, built into the wall near the two-story-high ceiling. Molly was on her own now; Gennie couldn't protect her after such a public display of defiance.

"Will you dance with us, Gennie?"

"What?" Gennie dragged her gaze from Molly and tried to focus on the speaker. Sister Theresa half stood, her arm curved outward toward the dancing area in the center of the room.

If she saw the mixture of emotions in Gennie's eyes, she was too polite to say so. She only repeated, "Will you dance with us? We will guide you in the steps, if you don't yet know them."

"Um, no, I think not," Gennie fumbled. She swiveled her knees to one side to allow Theresa to pass.

The sister nodded and made her way to the end of the bench. She took her place in a long, straight line of sisters which stood facing a shorter line of brethren across from the center of the room. All wore brand-new, pure white worsted Sabbathday outfits, fashioned over the past weeks by the tailors and seamstresses from patterns used in the 1830s. This was Wilhelm's idea, of course. He wanted to display the Believers' simplicity and purity. But to Gennie they looked as if they were all dressed up like ghosts for Halloween.

Gennie sat alone on her bench, too aware of the

hostile hiss of voices around her. She searched the room for someone friendly and saw two elderly sisters, too frail to dance, sitting together in the front row. To reach them, she would have to walk up five rows, all under the gaze of dozens of outsiders. Her feet refused to budge.

The six-voice chorus, three men and three women, began to sing a cappella and in unison. The first song sounded more like dance instructions than worship.

One, two, three steps, foot straight at the turn,
One, two, three steps, equal length, solid pats.
Strike the shuffle, little back, make the solid sound,
Keep the body right erect with ev'ry joint unbound.

Gennie knew the song well. Wilhelm had often used this march to teach Believers the square-order shuffle, one of the structured dances the Shakers developed soon after the early years of wild dancing worship.

"Might as well go to a square dance," a woman said.

"Just you wait, it'll git better. I seen the service last week," another, more knowing, voice answered.

After four repetitions, the song stopped. The line straightened and immediately the chorus began another brisk tune. This time the words were clearly Shaker.

Who will bow and bend like a willow,
  who will turn and twist and reel
In the gale of simple freedom,
  from the bower of union flowing.

"Here it comes," said the knowing woman. "This is a better dance, you wait and see."

Oh ho! I will have it, I will bow and bend to get it,
I'll be reeling, turning, twisting,
  Shake out all the starch and stiff'ning!

"Huh," the woman's companion answered. "Don't look like much to me."

Gennie bristled. She forced herself not to turn and frown at the women. She thought the dancing was pretty, if not very exciting. As the song spoke of "reeling, turning, twisting," the dancers made stylized, coordinated movements, bending from the waist in a way that seemed to represent reeling and twisting without actually doing it.

Each time the dancers bent, Gennie could see across to the men's side of the room, and to Grady. Now and then, he caught her eye, and once he gave her a careful half smile. But mostly his eyes darted around the room. She saw him look up at the Ministry's observation window, nod faintly, and move to the far corner of the room. She lost sight of him as the gentle dance quickened.

Rose frowned as Grady, on her signal, moved toward the edge of the room to keep an eye on Seth Pike. Seth stood off to the side, observing the dancers, his arms crossed tightly over his chest. He had never before attended a worship service, and Rose didn't like it.

"I do enjoy seeing the dancing again," Agatha said. She sat beside Rose at the observation window, high above the heads of the dancers. She leaned back in her rocking chair and pulled the lap rug tighter around her. "I haven't seen it so much since I was young. It makes me want to shake these old bones till the sins rattle out of them." She laughed softly. "Though I suppose I shouldn't tell that to Wilhelm. This is just what he wants, all the Believers singing and dancing again, like we used to."

Wilhelm wants more than singing and dancing, Rose thought. She noticed that Wilhelm and old Brother Hugo filled out the contingent of male dancers. But the sisters still outnumbered the brethren by at least two to one. What would they do if no new brethren joined the Society?

A few Believers were not dancing, Albert Preston, the carpenter, among them. He occupied a back bench on the edge of the men's side, near the door. Despite his strongly professed desire to become a Believer, he seemed uninterested in the dancing. His head moved constantly, as though the crowds fascinated him.

The chorus sang about bowing and bending like a willow, and the heads below Rose bowed and bent and twirled in lovely symmetry, like weaving on a winter loom. She was spellbound and for a moment wished that she, too, could dance with them.

The dancers' pace quickened. A few sisters twirled more and faster, their white skirts creating whorls in the moving fabric. Elsa's movements were more exaggerated than the others'. When the chorus sang of twisting, Elsa swiveled quickly from side to side. With each repetition of the song, she flung her body with more energy, so finally the sisters around her spread away to give her more room. Rose felt her stomach tighten.

"Agatha, can you see what is happening?" Rose asked.

Agatha opened her eyes and leaned forward to view the scene below. Rose peered over her shoulder. The third dance began. Once again the sisters prepared themselves, and the chorus burst into a spirited song.

Come dance and sing around the ring, live in love and union, and the dancers flowed into two circles, an outside ring of women around a smaller, inner ring of men, neither sex touching the other.

Sing with life, live with life, sing with life and power, sing with life, live with . . . The chorus stumbled to a halt. Inside the circle of dancers, Elsa bobbed up and down from the waist while she twirled feverishly, her skirt billowing out around her. Continuing to twirl, she leaned backwards with eyes closed and arms spread wide. Her clear voice broke the silence with an unfamiliar song in a minor key and then in no key at all. The lyrics weren't even words, but loud, guttural, meaningless sounds. Radiance gave to Elsa's plain features a contour and beauty that only Rose could see fully as she stared at the spinning face from her perch above the room. Other Believers writhed and shook around her.

Elsa stopped twirling and stretched her arms toward the ceiling. Then she crumpled from the waist, and her body shuddered as if she had thrown herself into a pool of ice water.

The dancers, recovered from their confusion, followed her lead. One by one, both men and women began to quiver and bend, forming a chaotic ring around Elsa. A sister, then several brethren, collapsed on the floor and writhed as if in agonizing pain.

In the midst of them, Elsa pulled herself upright again and stiffened her arms against her sides. She began to hop, her sturdy legs like coiled springs, thrusting her high off the floor.

"Wilhelm is responsible for this," Rose said somberly. "He warned us, remember? He has taken control of Elsa. We haven't done this kind of dancing worship for at least a hundred years, have we, Agatha? I've never seen it."

"Not since before I was born," Agatha said, very softly. "Oh, how I do wish it were real."

"This is part of Wilhelm's plan to take us backward in time, to make us strong again, *his* way," Rose said, anger tightening her jaw. "He has twisted Elsa into his image of the perfect Believer. He is using her to show the world how special we are. He believes they will beat down our doors to join us, if they just understand."

"They may indeed beat down our doors," said Agatha.

Rose turned quickly at the shakiness in Agatha's

voice. The eldress had shrunk back under her rug. One hand rested on the chair arm, its tremor noticeable.

"I should have let you rest after that lunch," Rose said. She reached over to touch Agatha's arm. "Don't be concerned, my friend," she said with gentleness. "That young deputy, Grady O'Neal, is down there, I've seen him. He'll see that nothing happens."

"One young man, what can he do?" Agatha sounded old and tired, worn out by her failing influence with Wilhelm. And by everything else, thought Rose, the Society's struggle to survive, her own declining health.

"The world is an evil place, Rose, and it is down there now. I can feel it."

Rose squeezed the thin arm. She never knew what to say when Agatha spoke of feeling evil. She never had feelings like that and very much feared that it was a requirement for being a good eldress.

Rose turned back to the observation window and anxiously scanned the room. The monitors had tried their best, but the room was filled to capacity and beyond. She located Gennie, sitting alone on the sisters' benches.

"I told her she could come," Rose mumbled. "Perhaps I shouldn't have. If anything happens to her, I'll never forgive myself."

Agatha said nothing.

"Oh dear, there's Molly," Rose continued. "And without her bonnet! I've protected that girl more than she deserves. Now it is time to be firm with her."

The eldress was silent. Rose turned to look at her friend. Agatha sat still, her eyes closed. In panic, Rose leaned close to listen for her breathing, but she could hear nothing over the music. Agatha's parchment face showed no flicker of movement. Rose eased the rug aside and lifted a frail, limp hand. She found a pulse so faint that she had to hold her own breath to feel it. For precious seconds, she was unable to speak or think what to do, willing her friend to be asleep only, not slipping away.

Gennie could not move. None of the stories had prepared her for the wildness, or for the fear and fascination that she felt watching it. She didn't wish to be part of it, not ever, yet its power held her.

A row of Believers dropped to the floor, and for just a moment Gennie stared over their heads into the faces of the world's men. A wall of loathing and revulsion stretched across the room, a vision more frightening even than Elsa's contortions. Instinctively, Gennie sought an escape route. The west doorway was invisible behind another wall of hate, this one female but no softer.

She hugged herself, trying to be as small as possible, while the mob of women swept past her, toward the dancers. Their Sunday finery kept all but a few younger ones from straddling the benches. Most of the women crowded around the edges of the benches, shoving into each other and rolling forward like molten lava.

Gennie caught the back of Molly's black head as she slipped through the crush and squeezed toward the door. If Molly could get out, maybe she could, too. She scrambled onto her bench and scanned the room. The men, too, were pressing toward the dancers, but faster than the women. They vaulted over the benches, clumsily toppling them on their sides.

"Witches! They're all witches, didn't I tell you?" Gennie heard behind her.

"I heard they run stark naked through the woods at midnight and worship the devil."

"They killed that boy, ya know. Reckon he was a sacrifice like, that's what my Joe said."

A few men yanked some ladder-back chairs and brooms from their wall pegs and held them above their heads.

Yet the dancers twirled and shook, unaware. Only

Elsa had stopped dancing, but not because she sensed danger. She stood rigid, surrounded by sisters and brethren, her hands stretched upward and her eyes squeezed shut.

"Gennie, run, get out now!"

Gennie strained her eyes in the direction of the command and saw Grady in front of the wall of men. He stood with his back to them, frantically waving at her. He was unaware that just behind him a man held a chair aloft by its legs.

"Grady, turn around," she shouted. "Turn around!" She stabbed her finger in the air toward the man, but Grady was too intent on getting her to leave. She watched, horrified, as the stranger ran toward the dancers. He swung the chair high above his head and smashed it down over the body of a brother kneeling in a quivering trance. The brother shuddered and crumpled to the floor.

The dancers around the fallen Shaker spun to a halt. A Believer leaned over to help his comrade, and another chair swung over both their heads. This time Grady saw it in time and threw his body against the assailant. The chair crashed harmlessly to the floor. But Grady's action triggered a burst of movement. Men jumped the last of the benches and piled into the center of the room, while the frightened dancers twirled now not in ecstasy, but in terror.

At the sounds of cracking wood, Rose slid the eldress's hand back under her rug and spun toward the observation window. The scene of violent chaos sent her reeling backward. She knelt quickly beside Agatha.

"I don't know if you can hear me," she said to the still figure. "But, please, my dear friend, please stay with us. I am going to get help."

She ran from the room, closing the door behind her in case some rioters should find the staircase. She rushed toward a small office on the same floor, which held the building's only telephone. Deeply as she loved the eldress, Rose's first call went to the Languor Sheriff's Office. It seemed forever before the operator connected her.

"This is Rose Callahan at North Homage," she said, gulping for air. "We need police help right away."

"Well, now, Miss Callahan, we ain't got much to work with just now."

Rose recognized the voice of the officer who had been less than sympathetic when the town boys had thrown rocks at their Plymouth.

"Send whatever you've got. Come yourself. And call Sheriff Brock immediately, tell him that a mob is attacking us. People are being hurt."

"Sheriff Brock's out at the Pike farm, and Grady's got the day off. I'm the only officer on duty, and I can't leave. I'll send someone as soon as—"

"This is an emergency!"

Rose clutched the receiver so tightly that her knuckles turned white. She forced herself to breathe slowly. "A friend is dying and I must call the doctor immediately," she said, fury lending her voice a clipped authority. "I don't have time to argue with you. Grady is here and could be hurt, too. Call Sheriff Brock and get over here. Now!"

Rose didn't wait for the officer to disconnect. She clicked the telephone cradle and dialed the Languor doctor's home phone number.

"Keep her warm," Doc Irwin said, "but don't move her. And, Miss Callahan . . . be prepared for the end. She's mighty weak."

Rose felt the tears fill her eyes as she replaced the receiver. *Not now,* she thought, *not now. Dear God, give me strength.* She longed to sit with Agatha, talk to her, hold her hand, be with her. But the Society needed her. Gennie needed her. She rushed past the closed door to the observation room, where Agatha sat still and alone.

* * *

The inner door leading from the smaller offices into the central meeting room was blocked by a mass of people. Rose exited through a small back door, then circled around to the front entrance. Some women fled the Meetinghouse, clutching screaming children. Molly's long, black hair swished across her back as she hurried in the direction of the Children's Dwelling House. A few other Believers had escaped, too, especially those who had remained seated in the back row during the dancing. An elderly sister supported another by the elbow. And the thin figure of Albert Preston headed in the direction of the Carpenters' Shop. *He might at least have stayed to help,* Rose thought. She squinted in the bright, warm sunshine and hunted for Gennie, but with no success. She must still be inside.

Rose straightened her back and elbowed through the crowd gathered at the west doorway.

"Step aside," she said with authority, "I've come to bring the children out. Let me through."

To her relief the group, most of whom were women, parted to allow her to pass. The next step, though, was harder. She had no idea what she could do once she was inside. Find Gennie and get her out, but then what? Could she get anyone else out? How long would it take for the police to arrive?

The room pulsed with quick-moving bodies creating much more chaos than the Believers' dancing could ever have done. Rose pushed into the room, slithering between people, grateful for her thinness. And for her height, which allowed her to see above the heads of most of the women and even many of the men.

She reached the center ring of spectators surrounding the dancers. Unlike the throng around them, these stood still, their attention on the dancing area. Their heads strained forward over each other's shoulders as if viewing a parade. Rose edged through them until she could see what they were watching.

It was not what she expected. She saw no trembling,

trancelike dancing. She could find neither Elsa nor Wilhelm in the scene before her. Both must have escaped. Instead, a tightly linked ring of sisters, their arms around each other's waists, knelt in a circle, facing inward. Their lips moved in prayer. This circle of bent figures surrounded and protected two hubs of activity. Inflamed as they were, these world's people hesitated to attack a wall of kneeling, praying women.

At one end of the enclosed circle, a cluster of the brethren tried to help their unconscious and wounded brother, the dancer who had been felled with a chair. Splintered chair legs and a slack woven seat lay near his limp body. Josie leaned over them, giving instructions. One of the men had taken off his own shirt and ripped it into strips. He wrapped one of these makeshift bandages around the victim's bleeding head.

At the other end of the sisters' protective circle, Gennie sat on the floor, her face streaked with tears. Using the white, triangular shawl from the bodice of her Sabbathday dress, she tried to wipe the blood from the face of Grady O'Neal as she cradled his head in her arm. No one stopped Gennie from touching him. Grady's eyes were closed and his body still.

SEVENTEEN

AS IF IN RESPONSE TO THE EVENTS OF THE DAY, gloomy clouds blanketed the late-afternoon sky. Rose wandered the grounds in back of the Meetinghouse, leaning now and then to scoop up a bit of trash left by the world. She could do nothing about the trampled and gouged grass. They would have to reseed.

Grady's head wound had bled badly, but it wasn't serious. Josie had bandaged him up and sent him home to rest.

Agatha, though, was in a coma. Rose had sat beside her in the Infirmary for two hours, until Josie ordered her out. She had promised to fetch Rose immediately if anything changed, but Rose feared that Agatha would open her eyes or even die, and she wouldn't be there. She fished a cigar butt out of the grass and tossed it into her nearly full basket.

"Rose."

She spun around to see Seth Pike, hat in hand, standing by the corner of the building. She dropped her basket and crossed her arms.

"Have you come to gloat?" All the anger that she had smothered throughout the attack on her people welled up inside her. "Or perhaps you'd care to throw something, or rip up a patch of garden. There's a bit over there that hasn't been destroyed."

Seth stared at the ground. He turned his hat slowly

by the rim and said nothing for a moment or two. He raised his eyes to Rose.

"I've come to say I'm sorry," he said in a halting voice. "I guess I wanted folks to get mad at you Shakers, but I never wanted nothin' like this to happen. You could've been hurt, and no matter what, I don't want that." He gnawed on his lower lip.

Rose wasn't finished being angry. "'No matter what?' Seth, we've done nothing to deserve this, nothing. Your mother made her own decision to join us, she came to us. We didn't entice her or force her. You're a grown man," she said harshly. "It's time you let your mother live as she wishes."

His face a livid red, Seth slammed his hat against the corner of the Meetinghouse. "Dammit, Rose, God dammit, I didn't mean my ma. She can go hop a freight for all I care, the old slut."

Rose took a deep breath to deliver a tongue-lashing.

"I meant *you.*" The anger drained from Seth's face, leaving it crumpled. "I meant you," he repeated softly.

A cloud darkened his face with shadow, concealing the lines etched by bitterness. For a moment, she saw the man he had been, young and determined and in love.

"That was so long ago," she said. "Seventeen years. Seth, we've lived another lifetime since then."

"Yeah, well, it ain't been much of a lifetime for me. The farm went to pieces, couldn't find a job, my ma's crazy, and my pa's not even my pa." He stared at the ground. "Never found another woman to love, neither. Not like you. Is it so wrong to love somebody?"

Rose had no answer to give him. She had spent many years trying not to think about him, even after he reappeared. Their time together had been so brief, less than a year, and they were both only eighteen. He had been her first and only human love. Now the Society was her only love. She had made the right choice, she knew that. But there were moments . . .

"I never meant to cause you pain. It wasn't easy to leave you, I want you to know that. But the call was so strong. Can you understand that? I belong here."

"Yeah." Seth flopped his damaged hat on his head and pulled at it to straighten it out. "Anyways, what happened today," he said, shoving his hands into the pockets of his Sunday-best pants, "I'm sorry. I won't bother you no more." He turned and walked toward the front lawn of the Meetinghouse.

"Seth, wait," Rose called. He turned to face her. "What do you mean, your pa's not your pa?"

Seth snorted. "I figured everybody knew by now. My ma ran around with our neighbor, Peleg Webster, the one Pa's been feuding with. Peleg's my real pa." He almost smiled. "One good thing, though. Peleg's leaving me his farm. That's why I'm back here. Maybe he's doing it to spite Pa, but that's OK by me. I get a second chance this way."

Gennie paced the herb fields, fidgeting and stewing. Rose hadn't said a word to her about tending to Grady after he'd been hit by a chair, which was almost worse than if she'd scolded. And where had Molly gotten to—again? Everybody else was busy cleaning up after the disastrous public worship service, so Gennie decided to search for her roommate. She'd start with their retiring room.

When Molly shed her bonnet at the worship service, it had looked like a declaration of independence, like she was planning to leave North Homage. If that were true, then some of her clothes should be gone. Her underthings, at least. Maybe she wouldn't want to wear Shaker dress outside of the community, but she wouldn't have much choice. She would need something to start with, as well as warm outer garments.

Gennie cut through the nearly empty kitchen garden. The kitchen door hung open as though someone had run through it and not bothered to push it all the way shut. Odd, she thought. Except on very hot days, Charity insisted that the door stay closed. She said it kept the baking more even.

Gennie stepped inside. For once, no one scurried around the kitchen. Plates of uncut bread and clean, empty soup tureens covered the center worktable, and a large kettle of soup bubbled furiously. She cut the flame under the kettle and stirred the thick liquid. The spoon scraped against a spongy layer stuck to the bottom. The soup had scorched. Charity must have heard all the ruckus at the Meetinghouse and fled the kitchen without a thought for saving the food.

She closed the door behind her and continued toward the Children's Dwelling House. The room was just as she had left it. No sign that Molly had returned in her absence. Gennie went straight to the storage drawers built into the wall and jerked Molly's open, one by one. She rifled through the contents with more urgency than care. She found enough undergarments to last until the next washday, and all of Molly's warm leggings. Her two work dresses hung on pegs, along with her everyday bonnet. So she must still be wearing her Sabbathday clothes.

Gennie grabbed the mattress on Molly's bed, but nothing had reappeared underneath. She must have hidden the things before coming to the service. And why did she come to the service, anyway? Nibbling on her lower lip, Gennie decided to check the deserted Water House. It was a logical place for Molly to hide.

The abandoned Water House, considered tempting and dangerous to children, was secured with a padlock on its only door. But Molly had met Johann here more than once. There must be a hidden entrance.

Gennie circled around to the back, where she found a small, low window, its latch hanging broken. That in itself was unusual. Normally Albert fixed broken doors and windows within a day or two. She pressed the window, and it creaked open. The space was just big enough for a slender person to squeeze through. The windowsill hit just above Gennie's waist. It looked clean. She stuck her head inside and searched the dim interior.

"Molly?" she called. *"Molly."* Her voice bounced off the two-story, kettlelike container that took up most of the building. The container used to provide the village's water but had been empty since they had installed modern plumbing. A narrow concrete walkway encircled the kettle. As she remembered, a metal stairway on the other side led both to an upper walkway and down to a crawl space, all designed to facilitate repair work.

Just beneath the window on the dusty floor, Gennie sighted a scuffed, dented object, small and tubular. It was the right size and shape for a lipstick container.

She hesitated to slip inside through the window. Though Molly could be hiding on the upper story or around the corner, the Water House was such a dank, cramped place to go for privacy, and Molly loved to be outdoors.

Still, she ought to rescue the lipstick, if that's what it was. She could show it to Rose. And she was curious about the crawl space. Wouldn't it be an ideal place to hide lipstick and powder and perfume?

She glanced back toward the fields and a dense grove of trees behind the Water House. She saw no one. She flattened her palms on the sill and jumped up, twisting to a sitting position. Gathering up the fullness of her skirts to keep from catching on any sharp edges, she slid one leg over the windowsill.

"What are you doing?"

The harsh voice stopped Gennie halfway through the window. Her heart pounding with guilty fear, she ducked her head back outside. Just at the corner of the building stood Albert Preston, his wiry body rigid, his eyes narrow slits in his bony face. He clutched his toolbox in one taut arm.

"Hello, Brother Albert, I—I'm looking for Molly. Have you seen her?" she finally managed to say.

"Building's locked up."

"Well, I . . ." Gennie was reluctant to mention the lipstick just inside. She hadn't even told Rose about Molly's mysterious beauty items yet. "It's just that I've looked everywhere else I could think of," she explained, sounding lame to her own ears.

"Nobody'd be in there," Albert said.

"But this window . . ."

"I'm about to fix it."

Gennie gave up. She slid her leg back through the window and slipped to the ground.

"Could you at least let me in so we could take a quick look around?" Gennie asked, shaking out her wrinkled skirt and moving hopefully toward the door.

"It wouldn't be right for you to go in there with me," Albert said sternly. He turned his back to her and began to inspect the broken window latch.

"I'll look later," he said, without turning around.

EIGHTEEN

DISAPPOINTED IN HER SEARCH FOR MOLLY, BUT EXcited by her glimpse of the object on the Water House floor, Gennie went in search of Rose. She found the trustee heading toward the herb fields and fell into step with her.

"You look like you could use a good ironing," Rose said, eyeing Gennie's wrinkled dress. "Where on earth have you been?"

Gennie swiped at her skirt. "Have you seen Molly? I've looked everywhere."

Rose sighed. "I'm sure she's about. I hope she's thoroughly ashamed of herself, too." She glanced sideways at Gennie. "I'm sorry, dear, I know you two are friends. But that girl is rebellious and troubled. Too troubled, I think, for you or me to help her."

"I'm scared for her."

"So am I," Rose said grimly. "But her soul is too twisted right now for anyone but God to help her."

"I don't mean her soul! I mean *her.* I'm scared for *Molly.* I'm afraid something bad has happened to her. Can't you understand? You just don't seem to understand anymore!" Gennie kicked at a rock in the grass and avoided Rose's eyes.

"I'm sorry," Gennie mumbled. "I didn't mean all that. It's just that . . . it used to be I could tell you anything, ever since I came here as a little girl. But now there are things . . . I don't know what's happening anymore."

Rose slipped her arm around the girl's shoulders. "It's time we talked," she said.

They strolled past the Herb House and into the fields. A few lacy clumps of fennel and coriander still struggled to form their seeds during the last sporadic warmth of the season. Ordinarily, Gennie loved to walk these rows, even when the harvesting was nearly done. But she might as well have been back in the kitchen, for all the pleasure it gave her now. She barely noticed the pungent rosemary, as she brushed against it upon entering the fields.

"Gennie?"

Gennie didn't respond. She wished she could take back much of what she had already said.

"My dear child," Rose began. "Nay," she corrected herself, "my dear friend. You aren't a child anymore, Gennie. You don't know how difficult it has been for me to accept that. I know I should love everyone equally, but you and Agatha are the two people I love most in the world. And I fear I am losing both of you. Nay, don't shake your head at me, we both know it's true. Agatha is failing, and you are growing up—and maybe away."

"But we'll speak more of that in a moment. First, Molly. Please don't think me heartless, but I do believe that Molly's soul is in much more peril than her body. I don't know where she has gone. Perhaps . . . perhaps it would be best if we never found out."

"Nay!" Gennie stomped hard on a clump of discarded basil root and a scattering of dirt flew out.

"Gennie, hear me out. The sheriff arrived as the service was ending, and we talked. He had found out—from others, not from me—that Molly and Johann had . . ."

"I know that they were together," Gennie said.

"Oh."

"Molly told me right after I found Johann. I promised her I wouldn't tell, and I had to keep my promise. You taught me that. And, anyway, what they did, that doesn't make her a bad person. It doesn't make her not worth looking for, does it? Anyway, I don't think so." She crossed her arms and rolled back on her heels.

"Of course she is worth looking for. But there's more that you don't know. Come on, let's walk."

Still frowning, Gennie strolled with Rose between rows of blackening plant stumps.

"Without my knowledge," Rose began, "the sheriff questioned Molly again. He's convinced that she killed Johann because he used her and then scorned her. The sheriff thinks that's probably why she ran off, because she knew he was getting close to the truth. You see, she was . . . with Johann . . . only a short time. Then he turned his attention elsewhere."

"Where?"

Gennie shot a sidelong look at Rose and waited to see how grown-up she really was in the older woman's eyes. A deep shadow passed overhead, followed by the far-off rumble of thunder. Rose glanced at the sky.

"All right, you don't have to tell me," Gennie said. "I know who it was. Charity."

"Did Molly tell you that, too?"

"She said enough for me to guess. Anyway, it was easy after seeing them look at each other at the Union Meeting."

"Of course, the Union Meeting. What else haven't you told me?"

Gennie folded her arms tightly against the growing wind and the edge in Rose's voice.

"Someone was giving Molly gifts or something," she said slowly.

"Gifts of what?"

"Well, things to make her pretty, like lipstick and perfume. I think I saw one of the lipsticks just now in the Water House, but Albert wouldn't go in with me to get it. And, also, she had a bunch of money. Maybe a hundred dollars."

"Money! Did Molly tell you that these were gifts?"

"Well, nay, just that someone gave them to her. I just thought . . . What else would they be?"

Rose walked silently, head bent. Another crack of thunder failed to distract her. Gennie hurried to keep up and watched her with growing concern. The information about Molly was important, that was clear. She should have told Rose sooner.

"There's more, too. Molly was out really late on Saturday night, and I went to look for her, and . . . Wilhelm found me and sent me back. He looked sort of sick, too, like maybe he wasn't sleeping well."

Frowning, Rose halted and stared down a row of gray-green lavender plants.

"Rose, are you mad at me?"

"What? Oh, Gennie, I'm sorry, I was just thinking, trying to understand . . ." With a slight shake of her head, she faced Gennie.

"Nay, I'm not angry with you," she said. "You have kept a great deal from me, but you did what you thought right." Her delicate face looked strained, her pale red eyebrows drawn together. "And I have not been completely honest with you, either. It is time that I told you a few things about myself, about my past."

The thunder rumbled closer now. There would be a downpour soon, and that would make it even harder to repair the trampled herb fields, but Gennie didn't care at that moment.

A spray of lavender stems had fallen to the ground during the harvest. Rose knelt and retrieved them. Twisting them absently between her fingers, she said, "Do you remember Seth Pike, the man I introduced to you at the market in Languor? He helps out with the farming chores, too, and he is Elsa's son."

Gennie nodded. None of this was new to her.

"When I was just a little older than you are, only eighteen, I left North Homage for about a year."

A few drops of rain splattered against Gennie's bonnet. She squinted to see Rose's face in the dim light.

"I'd been here since I was three, you see, so I'd never seen the world except those few tantalizing glimpses when Agatha took me into town for some errand or other. I used to make up stories for myself about the beautiful dresses I'd wear if I lived in the world, and the dances I'd go to. And about boys, how they would flock around me. So you see, I'm not so different from you. At eighteen I wanted to love and to be loved." Rose shook her head at her younger self.

"I met a young man, Seth Pike. He was gentle in those days, and eager for the future. We planned to marry. But I felt the call to come back, to become a Believer. It was so strong. I don't believe it was just guilt, I believe that God called me. So I left Seth."

"Did you tell Agatha that you wanted to leave the Society?"

Rose laughed. "Nay, I did not tell Agatha. Not until I decided for certain to leave. I didn't want to hurt her or lose her love." Rose looked intently down at the smaller Gennie.

"Gennie, you will never lose my love. Not ever."

"Not even if I leave, too? Even if I marry someday?"

"Maybe I'm not meant to be eldress," Rose said with a short laugh. "Sometimes these questions are too much for me. But, yea, even if you marry. I do truly believe that to be chaste is the higher calling, but I could never stop caring about you. And perhaps I'm not qualified to judge. I never married." She gazed steadily into Gennie's eyes. "But I was not chaste."

NINETEEN

MONDAY BROUGHT SUNSHINE BUT NO SIGN OF MOLLY and no improvement in Agatha's condition. Just before lunch, Rose closed her ledger books early to allow time for a visit to the eldress's bedside.

She bent and kissed the cool forehead. The eldress lay in an adult-sized cradle, tucked all around with a soft blanket as if she were a sleeping infant. Rose pulled up a chair and nudged the wooden cradle into a gentle rocking motion. Josie had said the rocking helped prevent bedsores. Rose hoped it would comfort.

"Are you feeling any better?" she asked. She spoke in a conversational voice, even though Agatha lay silent, deep in a coma. Rose wanted to believe that she could hear, even so. She rocked the cradle and gazed around the room. A bed and another cradle were empty, with fresh sheets and blankets pulled tight over them. They were alone. Rose slid her chair closer to Agatha.

"I wish you could tell me what to do, my friend," she said. "Sheriff Brock has issued a warrant for Molly's arrest. Gennie is convinced that Molly is innocent and in danger and that we should try to find her before the sheriff does. Perhaps she is right. Molly could have killed Johann, certainly. She was furious with him, and she is such an undisciplined creature. But I am having doubts." She frowned and leaned in closer.

"Gennie told me that Molly was receiving worldly

gifts, lipstick and so forth. That's what Gennie called them, gifts. But I don't think that's what they were. I couldn't say this to Gennie, she would become even more frightened for Molly, but it makes more sense to me that these so-called gifts were payment for something. Perhaps for carnal favors. Or perhaps for her silence."

A shaft of sunlight spilled through the window and shone on Agatha's unseeing eyes. Rose pulled the light curtains together.

"So, if Molly did not do the killing, we are left, I believe, with five people who had reasons to hate or fear Johann. Wilhelm knew him to be a fornicator who preyed on Shaker sisters, and Wilhelm's love for the Society is boundless. But I suspect there was more. He desperately wants Elsa to be the next eldress. He would then have almost total control over us, and we'd have no choice but to follow him."

Rose wandered to the window overlooking the medic garden. Too many possibilities bounced around in her mind, and she struggled to arrange them in a logical sequence.

"What if there is something about Elsa, something that could prevent her appointment as eldress," she said more to herself than to Agatha. "And what if Johann knew what it was? Sheriff Brock hinted that Elsa was unfaithful to her husband. Johann could have heard all sorts of rumors while he stayed on the Pike farm. Maybe there is something in her recent past or even her present that Elsa doesn't want known."

She began to pace the length of the cradle bed.

"Gennie said that she encountered Wilhelm in the cemetery the other night when she went out to look for Molly, and Molly's relationship with Johann could have given her the opportunity to learn what Johann knew. Might Wilhelm have been giving Molly gifts to keep silence about Elsa's past?"

"Elsa has the same reason to fear Johann. If he

revealed what he had learned about her, Elsa might never become eldress. And she does so want to be eldress." Rose heard the scorn in her own voice and tried to soften her tone. "Who's to say, maybe she should be."

Feeling suddenly self-conscious, Rose glanced at the open door of the sickroom. She got up and checked the hallway. It was still and empty, but just to be sure, she closed the door before continuing through her list.

"Charity could be involved, I'm sorry to say. I suspect that she had more of a relationship with Johann than she was willing to admit. She has been deeply troubled about something recently. And she could never risk being sent from North Homage; it might destroy her.

"Then there's Albert Preston," she said in a quieter voice. "We know so little about his past, and he was seen arguing angrily with Johann. His clothes were on Johann's body, remember.

"And finally, Seth Pike. I've added Seth to the list, Agatha. I know that won't surprise you." Rose laughed softly. "You never liked him, did you? Perhaps you were right. He rode the rails with Johann. They might have had a falling-out that he doesn't want us to know about. Albert found him hanging around the Herb House after the murder, too."

A dull pain was forming behind Rose's eyes. She settled back in her chair and rubbed her temples.

"You know," she said wearily, "something is eluding me. These five may have strong enough reasons to kill Johann, but why arrange his body in the herb-drying room? It just doesn't make sense."

The bell over the Meetinghouse chimed twelve times.

"It's time for lunch, Agatha," Rose said, "though even good Shaker food doesn't appeal to me just now. I've sent Gennie on an afternoon picnic with the children, so at least she'll escape from this for a time."

She leaned over Agatha's still face to kiss her good-bye. Each time she did so, she wondered if it would be the last.

"Perhaps I should not have told you all this. If you can hear me, it will only upset you, and you can do nothing about it. This time it's up to me. Rest well, my friend."

The apple orchard sparkled like a fairyland to Gennie, as the sun peeked through the broken clouds and glittered off the ripening fruit. Much as she loved the Herb House, she was glad to be outside and without work to do. True, she was to help supervise the children, but she didn't mind that. There weren't many of them, most went to orphanages these days, and they were mostly good children. Gennie liked children, which made her think about having her own, which made her think about Grady.

She helped Sister Charlotte shoo the children away from the unpicked fruit and toward an area of the orchard that was already harvested. They found a pleasant spot, dappled with the growing sunlight, and spread out blankets. Once they opened the large picnic baskets, the children gathered around, chattering and laughing.

"Ooh, I want some lemon pie!" said a seven-year-old girl who leaned over the basket as Gennie sorted through it.

"Sandwiches first, you know that, Nora," Gennie said, feeling grown-up.

Nora plunked down cross-legged on the blanket and kept her eyes on the pie pan, which Gennie placed out of reach of eager fingers.

After passing out sandwiches, Gennie leaned back against a tree trunk and gazed across the fields. She would have felt happy if a part of her weren't always looking for her dark-haired roommate. She slipped off her cloak and felt the warm breeze through her thin wool dress. She even dared to loosen her bonnet when she saw that Sister Charlotte had done so. Charlotte often made known her discontent with Wilhelm's desire to take Believers back to old-fashioned dress, and Gennie liked her for it.

The fields were harvested and empty for the winter, several tilled into neat rows, ready for spring, while others were still strewn with discarded plants. In the distance, Gennie saw a bundle of hay, which made her smile as she thought about the Halloween party they were planning for the children, with apple bobbing and a hayride. She hoped that they could still have the party, with everything that was going on. It would be good for the children. Rose said she wasn't sure how the Languor townsfolk would react, since they already thought that the Shakers were witches.

Something moved next to the distant hay bale. Probably one of the brethren cleaning up the field. Gennie squinted to see if she could make out a shape.

The figure moved away from the hay bale, and Gennie recognized the long skirt and bonnet of a Shaker sister. The woman staggered in a meandering path toward the picnic area. She tripped and fell to her knees, then struggled again to her feet.

As she drew nearer, Gennie saw that the woman wore a white dress, a Sabbathday outfit. Molly had worn such an outfit when she disappeared. She must be hurt. Maybe the killer had attacked her. Gennie jumped to her feet. But immediately, she saw that the woman was stockier than Molly.

"What is it, Eugenie?" Sister Charlotte sat on the opposite edge of the group of children, farther from the fields.

"I'm not sure."

Gennie felt a tug on her skirt and looked down at Nora's serious little face.

"It's the lady," Nora said, mumbling through a large mouthful of cheese and bread.

Gennie knelt beside the girl. "What do you mean, Nora? Nay, chew first, then swallow. That's a good girl."

"It's the lady. The lady!"

Gennie exchanged a puzzled glance with Charlotte.

"The lady I saw before." Nora scrunched her mouth in irritation at Gennie's slowness.

Snatches of a melody, sung by a powerful voice, reached the orchard. It was Elsa, her bonnet slipping to the side of her radiant face. She raised her hands, as she had in the dancing worship, and twirled joyfully, singing her own dance tune. Her cloth shoes were caked with mud. Her swirling feet kicked up clumps of rich, black dirt that splattered the edge of her once-white dress.

"Charlotte?" The alarm in Gennie's voice brought the sister to her side. "This is how she was at worship, did you see?"

"Yea, indeed," Charlotte said with clear disapproval.

"Is it a trance, do you suppose, or something else?"

"Something else, I'd say. Children, move back behind us now," Charlotte said, as Elsa twirled closer to the group. The children scurried farther back into the orchard, all except Nora.

"I saw her before," the little girl said with confidence, but she held tightly to Gennie's hand.

Elsa ignored everything but her dance. Gennie tore her eyes away and stooped again beside the child.

"Tell me where you saw her before," she said. Nora could not be describing the worship service because Rose had kept the children from attending.

Nora sucked in her lips and gazed up at Gennie through her lashes. "I wasn't supposed to be here," she said. "I was hungry," she added, as if that explained everything.

"You came to get an apple?"

Nora nodded.

"And you saw Sister Elsa?" Gennie prodded.

Nora nodded again.

"Did you see her out there in the fields?"

"Nay," Nora said, shaking her head widely side to side. "Here. She was singing and dancing with the trees, and that mean old man was here, too. He was watching."

"Nora," Gennie said, taking both the child's hands in her own, "who was the mean old man?"

As a girl-child, Nora had limited contact with the brethren, and Wilhelm, unlike his predecessors, ignored the children. Nora shrugged her shoulders.

"Was it the man with lots of white hair?" Gennie guessed. "Was it Elder Wilhelm?"

The girl flashed a front-toothless smile and nodded.

Elsa twirled to a halt and faced the group. Her dress was wrinkled and streaked with dirt, and straight gray hair escaped from her bonnet to hang in lank clumps across her cheeks. With an ecstatic smile, she stretched her hands toward them.

"I bring thee greetings," she said. "From Mother Ann herself!" Her voice had shed its coarseness and rang with a vibrant richness. She even sounded a little English, or what Gennie imagined to be English.

"I think Rose should know about this," Charlotte whispered. "I'm sending Hannah to the dining room to fetch her."

"Nay, she won't be there," Gennie said. "She told me she would try to talk with Wilhelm in the Ministry dining room. Maybe I should look for her."

"I need you here," Charlotte said, and turned to Hannah, a long-legged fourteen-year-old who looked more than willing to leave. "Try the Ministry House first," she told the girl. Hannah picked up her skirts and ran through the trees back toward the Ministry House, which lay just beyond the orchard.

Again, Elsa danced, edging closer and closer to the group. She twirled, then hopped up and down as she shouted nonsense syllables. The children huddled behind Charlotte and Gennie but peeked out with wide-eyed fascination.

Suddenly Elsa stopped and beamed at them. "I bring thee greetings and instructions from all the elders and eldresses who have ever lived," she said with majestic force. "They want thee to wait no longer. They want thee to see, to know, now, who I truly am!"

As Rose and Wilhelm neared the picnic area, they heard shouting and began to run. Rose's first thoughts were for Gennie and the children. She found them all facing the field beyond the orchard, the small figures clustered behind the protective backs of Gennie and Charlotte. Rose rushed to Gennie's side and followed her eyes to Elsa, planted ankle-deep in mud with her plump arms raised, palms open to the sky.

"Mother Ann, Mother Lucy, I hear thee! I am ready to reveal who I am. It shall be done according to thy wishes."

Wilhelm froze, his body taut, and stared at Elsa with fierce intensity.

"It must be clear to thee now," he said to Rose, "why Elsa will be our next eldress, and the task of gathering new souls must fall to thee. Elsa has been chosen. All the Believers who went before us have come to tell us that she is chosen to be the next eldress. Just as it used to be."

"It has been too long since Mother Ann spoke directly to one of us," he continued. "I myself have only read about it. I've never been so honored as to hear Mother herself speak to me."

Rose bit her lip. The reverence in Wilhelm's voice troubled her. She shivered, but not with awe. She, too, had read of the dreams and trances and messages from long-dead Believers. But it all happened so long ago. It seemed so strange to her now, in an age of locomotives and automobiles and telephones. She watched Elsa, with her dirty clothes, slouching bonnet, and face aglow with joy. The light in her eyes could be divine revelation. Or it could be madness.

As though sensing her scrutiny, Elsa dropped her arms and faced Rose. She held out one hand and walked directly toward the trustee. A prick of alarm shot through Rose, and her muscles tightened for flight. But she held herself rigid and waited for Elsa to reach her.

"Sister Rose," she said with quiet gentleness. "I have a message for thee, directly from Mother Ann." She smiled benignly and took Rose's hand.

"Mother wants thee, Rose Callahan, to be our next eldress."

Wilhelm's sharp intake of breath was the only sound to break the silence. Rose opened her mouth but no words formed. Her thoughts swirled in confusion. Secretly she had believed all along that Elsa's shaking and twirling served her own towering ambition, coached and nurtured by Wilhelm's passionate longing for a renewed Society of Believers.

Elsa dropped Rose's hand and paced back three slow, deliberate steps. Her hazel eyes, their yellow highlights flickering like flames, scanned the group, face by face.

"And now," she said, closing her eyes, "Mother Ann sends thee one more message. 'Listen,' she is saying to me, 'listen, my beloved children. The time has come, the time for which all Believers have hoped and prayed. Thy weakness is at an end. Thy strength shall bud and flower and shall glorify God and all who have gone before thee. It is many years since a strong and loving Mother has watched over thee and cared for thee. But now there is one among thee who is called. She will lead thee as I led, and Mother Lucy, as well. Follow thy new Mother, who shall serve thee even as she leads thee to health and strength and salvation. Greet her now. She is thy Mother Elsa!' "

TWENTY

GENNIE SLEPT FITFULLY, NEVER FAR FROM THE EDGE of wakefulness. The day had left her exhausted but agitated at the same time. Elsa as the new Mother? The very thought brought her out of sleep, counting the days until her eighteenth birthday, when she could leave North Homage. At least Rose would be eldress—if the Lead Society in New Lebanon, New York, approved, that is. Rose said she didn't know what they would make of Elsa's claim to be the new Mother. She thought they might wonder why Mother Ann had contacted Elsa herself and not someone else who could vouch for the authenticity of the call.

That Elsa might indeed be the chosen new Mother, Gennie did not believe for an instant. She had watched too much of Elsa's kitchen bickering. But something had certainly changed. Something important.

A chilly breeze from the open west window of Gennie's corner retiring room drifted across her face and left by the north window. She burrowed farther under her bedclothes and forced the day's events into a distant corner of her mind. Her breathing deepened.

A noise startled her awake, a faint crackling sound, like paper being bunched up in a ball. There was something familiar about the sound. She tried to identify it without stirring from her warm bed. In the night air, it seemed to come from right outside her window. She sat up and tossed her blankets aside.

"Molly? Molly, is that you?"

She heard only crackling, no voice, not even the call of a bird or a chirping cricket. The sound seemed to come from her left. As she reached her west window, the reason became clear. Inside the Water House, hungry yellow flames leaped from the ground floor to flashing peaks in the upper windows, devouring the old wooden outer structure.

A dark figure dashed past one ground-floor window. For a moment, the bright fire highlighted the outline of a long Shaker cloak. *It's Molly,* Gennie thought. *It must be. She's come back to rescue her things from the fire.*

She tore herself from the window and fumbled for her shoes and cloak. If no one else knew of the fire, she had to warn the village. The Water House itself was unimportant, but the clump of trees just beyond it could catch fire. If the wind shifted, the Carpenters' Shop and the Children's Dwelling House could be in danger. She raced to the hall telephone and jiggled the receiver. After endless moments, the operator finally came on the line. Gennie gulped the air to steady her trembling voice.

The Languor fire brigade alerted, Gennie careened down the stairs to the first floor and Sister Charlotte's room. She banged on the door and barged in.

"Charlotte, wake up! The Water House is on fire!"

Charlotte bolted upright and blinked rapidly, blinded by the sudden light from the hallway.

"I've called the fire brigade, and I'm going to ring the bell," Gennie continued. "Oh, please wake up quickly!"

"I'm awake." Charlotte tossed off her coverlet and flipped her legs over the side of her bed. "The children. I've got to move the children."

Gennie lunged for the front door. She had to reach

the old fire bell, next to the Meetinghouse. She raced in terror, as she remembered that the bell had been used only last Friday, when the barn burned. That was why the crackling sound had seemed so familiar to her. As she ran past the darkened buildings, she thought of shouting. But she had no breath to spare.

She tugged the rope with all her strength and set the old bell pealing loud and fast. Lights appeared in retiring-room windows. Gennie rang harder. As Believers emerged from front doors, still tucking in shirttails and fastening cloaks, she left the bell and flew down the central pathway, shouting hoarsely. At the Trustees' Office, Rose emerged from the front door and raced down the steps to meet her.

"It's the Water House," Gennie said between gasps. "I've called the fire brigade."

Rose nodded, her mouth set in a grim line. "I can see it from here. It's going fast. We'll have to form our own brigade to keep the fire from spreading."

Flames shot out from disintegrating walls and clutched at the old, dry wood of the abandoned building. Wilhelm stood at the head of the line, grimy sweat streaking his face. His powerful arms grabbed each bucket and hurled the water high at the flames. The blaze devoured bucket after bucket.

"More! Faster!" he shouted. The brethren were tiring. But Wilhelm seemed to gain strength as the fire worsened, as if this fire had ignited a rage inside him.

"Wilhelm, the fire brigade is on its way, and the wood is nearly all burned," Rose shouted as the fire began to burn out on its own.

Wilhelm tossed another bucket of water, which hissed and steamed as it encountered flame. He tossed the bucket to the ground and turned on Rose, his fists clenched into tight balls.

"The world has done this," he said in a ringing voice. No one moved.

"This is the work of the world," Wilhelm repeated, "first our barn, and now this. And they will be back to try again. They will not rest until they have destroyed us. Is it now finally clear to thee, to all of thee, that we can *never* compromise with the world?"

No one slept that early Tuesday morning. The first pink stripes of dawn found everyone cleaning bits of charred wood from the grounds, edging closer to the black hulk that used to be the outer structure of the Water House. The water tank itself was soot-covered but intact. Everything around it had burned away, except the metal staircase and the stone floor.

Rose poked at a blackened chunk near the building and watched for sparks. She bent to pick it up. It was cold and soggy and left a sooty residue on her hand. Crinkling her nose, she tossed it aside and wiped the muddy ash on her apron.

Two young boys scrambled over the charred shreds that used to be the wall to explore the floor of the building. Rose recognized them as rebellious friends, aged ten and twelve, always on the lookout for whatever trouble they could get into. She glanced around her and saw everyone else retreating toward the dining room for breakfast.

The older boy tested the temperature of the water tank with one finger, then laid his palm flat on it and gestured to his friend. Both boys tried the stair railing and found it cool enough to hold. They peered into the crawl space. Rose couldn't see the expressions on their faces, but their bodies said enough. They wanted to explore.

"You two," she called. "Come out of there. It's time for breakfast."

For a moment she thought the boys would defy her, but hunger won. They scrambled out of the ruin and raced each other to the dining room.

Rose stood alone on the outer edge of the charred

walls. She could see the metal stairs spiraling down into the dark hole of the crawl-space opening. As she turned to leave, something about the glow of the morning sun made her remember what Gennie had told her about the lipstick cover inside the Water House. Surely Molly must have used the building, probably the crawl space, as a hiding place for her beauty items. What if she hadn't been able to rescue them last night? What if they were still there, just down that dark hole?

Catching her skirts and cloak up in a bunch, Rose stepped over the ragged, blackened remains. The stone floor seemed stable enough. A few more steps brought her to the edge of the crawl space. Perhaps Molly had more down there than just lipstick and perfume. Maybe she could find a clue to the source of these secret gifts of hers.

She leaned over the edge of the opening and squinted into the dimness. The sunlight formed a gray circle on the dirt floor, surrounded by black, acrid air. Rose saw nothing sparkling in her field of vision, but Molly surely stuffed her treasures into one of the dark corners of the crawl space.

Rose reached for the iron stair railing and tested its stability. It stood firm. She dropped her cloak in a heap on the sooty, stone floor, then gently swung around to the first step and lowered herself into the crawl space.

Her feet touched ground, but her head still stuck out of the opening. She would have to squat down in the dark to look around. Though she knew every inch of North Homage and had been down in the crawl space as a child, she felt a quick stab of uneasiness. She thought about rats. But they'd be dead from the fumes, if not the fire itself, she told herself.

Rose closed her eyes and knelt down, lowering her head under the crawl space ceiling. She eased open her eyes. She could see little of the crawl space beyond the area lit by the opening. The air felt clammy. The scorched smell was milder than she'd expected. The fire must have spared the crawl space.

She chose a direction at random and, using her hands like antennae, edged into the darkness. Her hands encountered chunks of wood, a hammer, debris from years of use and repair. Gradually, her eyes adjusted so that she could begin to see shapes a few feet ahead of her.

The floor creaked above her. She froze, every muscle taut. Was the flooring above her solid all the way across? Was someone up there? Her imagination, usually so well controlled, raced through several terrifying possibilities, leaving her paralyzed on hands and knees.

Finally, the silence reassured her. She shook her head at her own susceptibility and pushed forward. She had come within sight of one wall. Her eyes traveled down the wall and into the dim corner where it joined the floor. Something was there, partly in shadow. Her fears forgotten, she crawled forward and grabbed it. She held a dusty mother-of-pearl handle attached to a metal nail file. It had to be Molly's. No one else in North Homage would own such an object.

She reached into the shadows and felt for more shapes. She found them. One lipstick, dented but otherwise whole, and a lavender perfume bottle. She stuffed the items inside the triangular kerchief that covered the bodice of her dress and felt around once again. She found nothing more.

More than ready to leave, she twisted around to locate the gray spot under the crawl-space opening. Her eyes were now thoroughly adjusted to all but the dark edges. As her gaze swept across the area, she could just make out the dozens of items that had been tossed down over the years. Most of them looked broken or worn—a rusty handsaw, three screwdrivers, a paintbrush with bent bristles, just peeking out of the deep corner shadows. Nothing, though, that looked like clues to Molly's behavior or disappearance.

Rose's eyes snapped back to the paintbrush with no sign of paint on its dark bristles. Bristles bent like soft hair. She forced herself to edge closer. A shape formed in the shadow. Molly lay facedown in the dirt, her glorious black hair tossed over her head as if she were about to run a comb through it one last time, her arms and legs twisted unnaturally. A boneless rag doll tossed thoughtlessly into a dark closet.

A small cry escaped her own mouth and Rose started, as if it had come from someone else. She whispered Molly's name. No answer came from under that riot of black hair.

The damp, bitter air pressed on the somber group gathered around the ruined Water House. The county fire brigade had returned and ripped away the floor over the crawl space. Sheriff Brock and Grady stood upright in the area where Molly Ferguson lay still. The Languor physician gently lifted the girl's hair and examined her head and neck. With light, probing fingers, he touched the bruises around her eye.

"Yea, it is Molly Ferguson," Rose said, as the doctor raised his eyebrows in a silent question.

The police and the doctor closed ranks. They talked quietly among themselves, leaning over to see where the doctor pointed. Rose eased forward to hear what she could. She caught only a few phrases, something about bruises around the girl's neck.

Rose guessed the rest. Molly must have been strangled, either in the Water House or elsewhere before being dumped in the crawl space. Dumped. As if she were a pile of dead plant stumps. Rose was furious with herself. She had been so ready to believe that Molly had run away and that her soul was in more danger than her body. Hubris.

Molly had not killed Johann, that much was clear to

her. She probably died because she knew who did. And whoever killed Johann had now compounded his sin unimaginably. Perhaps God could forgive him—or her—but Rose could not. Not yet. Sheriff Brock could try to shut her out of this, but it would make no difference. With or without the help of the police, she would find out who had done this, even if it were a Believer. Especially if it were a Believer.

The doctor finished his examination and touched the still-intact black hair with one tender stroke. The gentleness broke through the protection of Rose's anger. She blinked rapidly and brushed away the tears that clustered on her eyelashes.

She picked her way over chunks of charred wood to get closer to the group.

"Found these in the rubble on the ground floor," Grady said, opening his palm, in which Rose saw two blackened objects. "The compact was open and the insides burned out, and the lipstick was pushed all the way up before it got knocked off or the fire melted it. She could have been putting some lipstick on when she was attacked."

"Sad," Doc Irwin said. "She may not have expected any attack. Aside from those neck bruises, there are no obvious signs of a struggle. But we'll know more after the autopsy. It's amazing that the fire didn't get to her and cause more damage."

"That'll be a disappointment for whoever killed her, more'n likely," Brock said. "He could of thrown gasoline on her, that would've done it." Brock turned and narrowed his eyes at Rose. "Maybe the killer was someone that didn't know much about killing and getting away with it. Like one of y'all."

Grady flashed a look at Rose that she interpreted as "Don't say anything right now." She clasped her hands in front of her and clamped her lips shut. Wilhelm, too, remained unusually silent, so absorbed that he failed to notice that he stood too close to Rose. She moved a few paces aside. Wilhelm's jaw muscles tightened and flexed and tightened again. Dark smudges under his eyes betrayed his strain.

"Want me to start questioning folks?" Grady asked, taking out his notebook and pencil stub.

"Yeah, you bet. 'Specially him," Brock said, jerking his head toward Wilhelm, "and that crazy Elsa Pike. Word is she's gone off the deep end with this shaking stuff. Could be she took vengeance on the girl for runnin' around. Wouldn't put it past her." Brock warmed to his theory. "Maybe she decided that if she couldn't run around no more, nobody else could neither. Like one of those teetotaler temperance ladies."

"You," Brock said to Rose, "stay away while Grady takes those statements. Y'all stick together too much. I want you to stay out of this, understand?" Rose saw in his taut face and narrowed eyes that he was ready to end this case, one way or another. She said nothing, promised nothing.

Two men from the fire brigade lifted Molly out of the opened crawl space and over the blackened stumps that once were walls. Her long, dark hair rippled beneath her as they laid her on the singed grass. Her white Sabbathday dress was streaked with dirt and soot. Rose sighed a prayer as she turned away.

TWENTY-ONE

ROSE PACED HER OFFICE UNTIL THE POLICE LEFT. SHE watched their black Buick spin up dust, threw her cloak over her shoulders, and cut through the village to the Ministry House. Without knocking, she burst into Elder Wilhelm's office. Wilhelm knelt on the floor beside his writing desk. His head snapped up.

"How dare thee interrupt me at prayer."

"There is no other time, Wilhelm. Is this what you wanted? Is this the way you wanted it to turn out? Two people are dead, one just a girl."

"It was the world," he said, "this is all the world's—"

"Nay, Wilhelm, not the world. A *person* has done this. Maybe a Believer. I'm sure you told the police nothing useful, but I am not the police, and I insist on the truth. Finally, Wilhelm, tell me the truth, before any more lives are lost."

Wilhelm remained kneeling. Rose noticed that he had left the shutters drawn over his long office windows as if he couldn't bear the sunlight. A small desk lamp showed the slow flush traveling up Wilhelm's neck and face. With one burly arm on the smooth oak surface of his desk, he pulled himself to his feet. For a moment his eyes flashed, and Rose wondered if he would strike her, but instead he crumpled, as if someone released a valve and all the angry steam hissed out.

He dropped into his chair and leaned on his desk, his forehead in his hands. Rose eased into a ladder-back visitor's chair to give Wilhelm time to compose himself.

"I think I know what has been going on with Elsa," she said. "You've been molding her into your image of the ideal eldress, haven't you? An eldress who would give us new energy, who'd lead us forward by turning us backward. You taught her about dancing and shaking, speaking in tongues and going into trances. That was what the little girl, Nora, saw in the orchard, wasn't it? A training session!"

"Nay, that isn't true!" Wilhelm's head popped up and a lock of white hair fell across his forehead. "Elsa has the gifts, she does, but she had so little . . . experience. I was merely helping her understand, teaching her." He held out his hands, palms upward.

"But now the pupil has overwhelmed the teacher," Rose continued quietly. "Elsa has found a way to surpass even you. By declaring herself the new Mother, Elsa will follow in Mother Ann's footsteps. Mother Ann would never, ever have condoned such behavior. You know that, Wilhelm."

Wilhelm's face sagged. He looked far older than his sixty years.

"In the end," Rose added softly, "Elsa would be more honored than you. Did you anticipate that when you made your plans?"

Elsa was a clever woman. Or was she? Rose had seen those firelit eyes. Perhaps she had absorbed Wilhelm's lessons so well that she truly believed herself to be chosen. Perhaps she had gone over the edge.

A distant bell rang, calling Believers to evening meal, but Rose didn't budge. Wilhelm rubbed his puffy eyelids, then slowly opened them.

"Elsa was practicing," he said in a weary voice. "I thought she learned so very quickly, she must indeed have the gifts. But she practiced on her own at night.

Johann saw her. He understood that her movements weren't real, that she was pretending. After he told me what he had seen, I went out for several nights to watch for myself."

"Is that why you were out Saturday night when you found Gennie at the old cemetery?"

Wilhelm nodded. "Even after Johann's death, I followed Elsa every night. I saw her dance, heard her speak in tongues. I wanted it to be real. Sometimes it did truly look real, and I was convinced, but then . . ."

"So Johann threatened to tell the Society that Elsa was a fake. He blackmailed you."

"Nay!" Wilhelm pounded the desk. "He tried, first Elsa, then me. Neither of us gave in to his vile demands for money."

"Yet he didn't tell anyone about Elsa. Why not?"

"Because he had no chance. He was killed that same night." Wilhelm sank back in his chair. "But neither I nor Elsa had anything to do with that. I swear by all I believe in."

"How can you be so sure about Elsa?"

Some of the old power lit his tired eyes. "I know."

"Just as you knew that she had the gifts?"

Rose missed dinner, but she cornered Gennie as she left the dining room.

"Come with me to the Herb House," Rose said abruptly. "I need to know what was in that bouquet you saw on Johann's chest."

"You believe me!"

"I should never have doubted you."

They hurried through the kitchen garden and backyards to the Herb House. Once in the second-floor drying room, Rose pushed Gennie toward the worktable where she'd found Johann. The table had been scrubbed clean of any dirt from Johann's body. One bunch of lavender lay on the corner, its dried buds deep purple in the sunlight from the window.

"Think now," Rose urged. "What did you see? Close your eyes and imagine the scene, even if it frightens you. I think this is important."

Gennie removed the lavender and stared at the empty table. Then she shut her eyes tightly and sucked on her lower lip.

"I don't know, I was so upset, I—"

"You called it a bouquet. A bouquet usually has flowers in it. Think, Gennie, were there flowers in it? Was it all brownish or were there colors?"

Gennie's face scrunched up for several moments, then cleared as her eyes popped open.

"There were colors! I'm sure of it. Lavender, I think. And orange or maybe a dark yellow. Green, too, of course—a strong green."

She smiled expectantly, but Rose was puzzled.

"Green?" Rose asked. "But I thought you said the bouquet was dried." She glanced around her at the hanging bunches of oregano and lemon balm and tarragon hanging from the rafters. Some retained a pale green, but most turned brown when they dried.

Gennie frowned and closed her eyes again.

"Take yourself back to that morning," Rose said. "Let your mind wander through the rows of hanging herbs, past the drying tables covered with smaller herbs, then you come upon Johann's body." Gennie winced but Rose continued. "Now focus on the bouquet, see the bit of string binding the sprigs together. Look at the bouquet itself, the colors. Can you identify the herbs?"

Gennie began hesitantly. "I think the orangy color was a calendula, or maybe two, an orange and a yellow. They were dried, I'm positive, and the lavender looked shriveled." Her eyes flew open. "I've got it! I remember! The green was rosemary, lots of rosemary, maybe even four or five sprigs."

"Rosemary does turn pine green when it's dried,"

Rose said. "Are you certain now that those were the herbs you saw?"

"I'm definitely sure. I can recognize practically any herb, dried or not," Gennie said. "I can tell catnip from anise hyssop, even without smelling them. Molly tested me once, and I always—"

"What is it?"

"I'm just remembering . . . you said pine green, and it wasn't pine green. It was bright green."

"We haven't harvested any rosemary for at least three weeks," Rose said. "What we harvested has already turned dark. Someone went to the trouble of picking fresh rosemary sprigs for Johann Frederick's funeral bouquet. But why?"

Before dawn on Wednesday, Rose absently rocked herself in the small sitting room connected to her retiring room. Time grew short. Already, the town of Languor knew of Molly's murder. They blamed the Shakers. After helping Gennie dredge up her memories about the bouquet, Rose had escorted the girl to her retiring room past a group of rowdy young men, who cursed and threatened them. Rose had sat up all night after that, watching over her village, her mind racing to fit the pieces together.

Someone had picked fresh rosemary, mixed it into a dried herb bouquet, and left it on a murdered man's chest. The fresh rosemary carried a message, it had to, or else why bother? But why would the killer bother to send a message at all? It must have something to do with the Society, maybe something in their past.

She glanced at the small, plain desk in the corner of her sitting room nearest the window. Faint pink light had begun to spread across its clean pine surface. Her personal journals lined up neatly beginning at the left corner with 1920, the year Rose had returned to North Homage and signed the covenant. She retrieved the sixteen-year-old journal and slid into her small, slat-backed desk chair. Without much hope of finding an answer but desperate for something to trigger her sluggish thinking, she began to turn the yellowing pages. She scanned snatches of her own youthful handwriting whenever she saw mention of rosemary.

She had noted that the rosemary crop was good that year. Tins of Shaker dried rosemary had sold well in the world. During her kitchen rotation, she had experimented with various combinations of herbs in breads. One recipe for rosemary muffins had been so popular that she'd written it out in her journal. The recipe had been used by the kitchen sisters until Elsa had taken over the breadmaking and dropped the use of herbs.

Rosemary's Muffins

Beat together one large egg (fresh) with one cup milk and 1/4 cup butter, melted. In a separate bowl, mix together 2 cups of flour with 1/4 cup sugar, 1 Tablespoon baking powder, and 1 teaspoon salt. To the dry mixture, add 1 Tablespoon fresh rosemary, 2 teaspoons fresh thyme, and 1/2 teaspoon rubbed sage. Stir egg mixture into dry ingredients until moist but still lumpy. Bake in moderate oven until the tops are golden brown. Makes a dozen muffins and will feed 12 sisters or 6 brethren.

Rose squinted at the recipe in the dim light. Rosemary's muffins? She was certain she'd meant to name them "Rose's Rosemary Muffins." A silly error. That's what comes of writing too fast and not concentrating.

She started to turn the page, but her hand stopped in midair. She saw herself as she had been when she'd written those words. She was nineteen, a new Shaker sister, determined to strive for perfection in her new life and to atone for the mistakes of her past. More than anything, she had vowed to reject any thoughts that bound her to the world she had left. But some memories wouldn't be killed so easily. Her silly error was, in fact, a reminder. Rosemary for remembrance. She remembered, and a piece of the puzzle fell into place.

Dawn light splashed on the stairs as Rose slipped down to the Trustees' Office and placed a call to the eldress of the Hancock Society in Massachusetts. After a night of thinking and very little sleep, she decided it was time to test one of her ideas about why Johann Fredericks had been murdered. She needed some information, and the eldress might be able to help her.

After a frustrating delay, the operator reached a soft-voiced sister in Massachusetts. The eldress had just arisen, she said, and would take several minutes to come to the phone. Rose closed her eyes and touched cool fingers to the lids to ease the burning.

At a rustling sound, Rose turned to see Josie, the infirmary nurse, framed in the doorway. She smiled.

"Agatha is coming back to us," she said.

Rose dropped the phone back on its cradle and ran the distance to the Infirmary.

Rose clutched the edge of the cradle bed and searched Agatha's chiseled face for signs of life.

"I'm only sure that she's come out of the coma," Doc Irwin said. "For the rest, we'll have to see." He reached out as if to offer Rose a comforting touch. Remembering who she was, he withdrew his hand.

Josie offered what the doctor could not, a hand on Rose's shoulder.

Sister Theresa burst into the room, panting and red-faced. "Oh, Rose, I'm so sorry to interrupt, but something awful is happening. You've got to come quickly. The sheriff's here and he has arrested Elsa! He actually forced his way into the sisters' side of the Center Family House. Wilhelm is furious, I'm afraid of what might happen . . ." She saw the faint color in Agatha's cheeks and gasped with pleasure.

"I'll be there in a moment," Rose said quietly.

Theresa looked over Rose's head at Josie, who gave a slight nod and led the way. Theresa and the doctor followed, closing the door behind them.

In her relief, Rose no longer felt her lack of sleep.

"Agatha, my old friend," she began, as she had since the eldress had lost consciousness. Agatha's eyelids flickered but remained closed.

She reached over and placed her hand over Agatha's where it lay on the coverlet. Her skin was warm, but it would be a long time before Agatha would truly be back with them. She might never return completely. Rose said a prayer of thanks to God, and to Mother Ann for interceding on Agatha's behalf.

Rose did not go immediately to the Center Family House. Instead, she placed her interrupted phone call to the eldress at the Hancock Society in Massachusetts.

Gennie hadn't been able to sleep, either. After a night of twisting her sheets off the bed, she slipped into her clothes and set out for a prebreakfast walk. She hurried past the burned-out Water House, holding her breath to avoid the damp, sour smell of the ruined wood. She reached the small patch of woods beyond the Water House. The trees remained blessedly untouched by the fire. If Molly had made a habit of going to and from the Water House, she might have hidden in these woods.

Gennie covered the small area twice and found nothing. She wasn't even sure what she was looking for. Some sign of Molly's presence, some reminder of her life, or clue to her death. Mostly, she was just moving to keep from feeling overwhelmed by her own regrets. If only she had told Rose sooner about Molly's secret stash and her tryst with Johann in the Water House. Maybe she wouldn't be dead.

Returning to the edge of the woods, Gennie gazed beyond the charred Water House to the Carpenters' Shop and the path that ran through the center of North Homage. The Children's Dwelling House stood just east of the Carpenters' Shop. Molly could easily have reached these woods from their retiring room. Smoothing her cloak under her, Gennie dropped down cross-legged on the damp ground, her chin on her knuckles.

No one could have slipped Molly's body into the crawl space after the fire. The building was never out of sight of several Believers between the time the fire ended and the discovery of her body. She was in the crawl space, dead or dying, before the fire began. So who was it Gennie had seen running in front of the burning Water House?

Had the running figure started the fire? But if that was someone from Languor, as Wilhelm insisted, would the person have worn a Dorothy cloak? Rose said that people from the world had worn them once, but they were out of fashion now. Unless she wore the cloak to throw suspicion on the Shakers. Or maybe it had indeed been a Believer who ran in front of the burning building, and maybe she killed Molly, too.

Gennie thought back to the night of the fire. Despite the cloak, the figure had looked like a slender girl, quick and lithe. Elsa was stocky and bore down heavily when she walked. But it could have been Charity or any of the younger sisters.

The back door of the Carpenters' Shop opened and Albert Preston emerged, holding a heavy-looking pail. He dumped some dirty water on the ground near a pile of scrap wood. Gennie glanced above his head and saw a second-floor window with a thin white curtain draped across the inside. Of course, she thought, springing to her feet, Albert lives right upstairs. Maybe he saw something that night. Maybe he doesn't even know that it's important. She started toward the shop as Albert let himself back indoors.

Wilhelm, a white lion with muscles bunched for attack, stood between Sheriff Brock and Elsa Pike, as Rose approached the group on the road just outside the Trustees' Office. They had allowed Elsa to dress, but her gray hair poked out the edges of her white cotton cap. The sheriff wore his catlike look again, as though he had what he wanted and could afford to wait for it to yield. He shoved his hat farther back on his head and brushed open the side of his jacket so everyone could see his undrawn gun. With his other hand, he reached inside his pocket and withdrew a folded piece of paper.

"We got ourselves a warrant, Mr. Lundel. Nothin' you can do about it, so you might as well step aside."

Wilhelm held out his hand for the warrant.

"Now, Mr. Lundel, this here's legal stuff."

"We know a great deal about legal matters."

Brock handed over the warrant. Wilhelm scanned it and tossed it back.

"This is persecution," he said, crossing his thick arms over his chest.

Brock's thin body tightened, his half smile undimmed.

"Like I said, Mr. Lundel, nothin' you can do about it. We got the law on our side. Come on, Elsa, step around here. Come easy and we won't handcuff you."

"Stay still, Elsa." Wilhelm's bushy white eyebrows joined in a fierce line over his smoldering eyes.

"Now look here, Lundel, don't you interfere none. Besides, y'all ain't supposed to be violent, the way I hear it."

"Elsa, come forward, we have no choice," Rose said, taking Elsa's arm.

Elsa shook off her hand. "Address me as Mother."

Rose counted the silent seconds and watched Elsa's plain features redden as it became clear that Rose would not call her Mother.

"The sooner you go," Rose said so quietly that only Elsa could hear her, "the sooner we can telephone our lawyer to help you. Do you wish for Wilhelm to break his vow of nonviolence and perhaps be hurt?"

Elsa hesitated. With a doubtful look at Wilhelm's stolid back, she stepped forward.

"Don't you take my ma away!" Seth Pike came running from the direction of the herb fields, his hat in his hand. "She didn't kill anybody!"

"Sorry, Seth," Brock said, "but we got reason to think that your ma murdered Johann Fredericks on account of him knowing about her past and all."

"That's crazy. They'd have forgiven her for her past, wouldn't you, Rose? Tell him." Seth crumpled his hat in his hands and appealed to Rose. She nodded slowly.

"If she confessed to the eldress and lived a pure life from then on out, yea, she'd be forgiven," she said. "Believers have been forgiven for much worse transgressions, committed even after signing the covenant."

"She confessed to me," Wilhelm said. Rose spun around in astonishment. For a sister to confess to an elder, rather than one of her own sex, was not their way.

"There, you see," Seth said. "She didn't have no reason to kill Johann."

Brock shook his head and kicked at the ground with the toe of his boot. His grin widened. "Well, you see, Seth," he said, "that ain't all. Your ma, she's been acting crazy lately, having seizures-like and hearin' voices. The way we figure it, Johann threatened to spread the story of her runnin' around, maybe he said he'd tell everyone in North Homage, so's she'd be a laughingstock and nobody would want her to be their priestess or whatever. So she stabbed him and buried him for a while till she could get things set up, then she carried his body to the Herb House—she's a sturdy hill-country woman—and she did some kind of ritual-like on account of his spirit being unclean or whatever. That's the way I figure it."

His listeners were stunned to silence by this theory. Even Grady looked embarrassed.

"Grady, handcuff Elsa," Brock ordered. "Lundel, you step aside now." The sheriff swept aside his jacket and held his hand just above his gun.

"Sheriff," Rose said sharply, "there's a flaw in your theory."

Brock jerked his head toward her. "Yeah? What's that?"

"We Shakers have no history of doing any sort of purifying herb rituals over the dead."

"Yeah, you said that before, but like I said, Elsa's crazy."

"Yet all Elsa has done is dance as Shakers danced long ago. She slips into trances and speaks in tongues and hears messages from long-dead Believers, just as early Shakers did. Everything that she has done, everything you call crazy, is part of our history. Why would she suddenly do something so completely foreign to us as a purifying ritual for the dead? Why, how would she even have heard of such a thing? It isn't done around here anywhere that I know of."

Brock hesitated. He wasn't buying her argument, she could tell, but she had planted one little seed of doubt in his mind. She glanced over at Grady, who gave her a slight nod and raised his eyebrows as if to ask, "who then?"

In response to the unspoken question, Rose asked one of her own. "What if the murder and the placing of the body in the Herb House were done by two different people?"

Now she had Brock's full attention. "Go on," he said, dropping his hand away from his gun.

"Well, what if the two acts were done for different

reasons? Johann's killing may have been a matter of expediency. Maybe he knew something or was blackmailing someone, and that person wanted to be rid of him."

"And Molly?" Sister Josie asked softly.

"I suspect that Molly found out who killed Johann and conducted her own version of blackmail. You've all heard by now about the money and beauty items that Gennie found under Molly's mattress and again in the Water House. My guess is that those were payments from Johann's killer for Molly's silence. But finding Johann in the Herb House, that didn't make sense to me. Not until just recently, when I was reminded of long-ago times." She turned to Seth. "You moved Johann's body, didn't you?"

Seth jutted out his chin in defiance before bowing his head.

"Yeah, all right," he said. "That was my doing. But I didn't kill him, I swear to God." His voice broke, and he took a moment to steady it. "I couldn't sleep one morning, so I went out to work before everyone else even got up. I cut through a field next to the Herb House, one that got harvested early and tilled under way back before I got to town. Most of the dirt was crusted over, but there was this one area that felt soft, like it just got dug. Seemed funny to me. I had a shovel with me, so I dug down a bit. And that's how I found him. Me and Johann, we weren't getting along so good at the end. He even tried to get money out of me. He threatened to tell Peleg Webster that Ma wasn't sure he was my real father. Then I wouldn't get Peleg's farm. That farm's my chance to make something of my life. So I wasn't all broke up about finding him dead. But I sure was spooked. That's what gave me the idea—feeling spooked."

"So you carried him to the Herb House?"

Seth nodded. "At first all I thought was to get the police. I ran clear past the Carpenters' Shop before I got this idea. That's when I saw those clothes hanging out. I grabbed them and run back. I switched his clothes so he'd look like a Shaker."

"Where's his real clothes?" Brock asked.

"I sneaked them back to my pa's farm last market day. Buried them in one of his fields."

Seth twisted the rim of his misshapen hat. "I've been mad ever since I saw you again, Rose, that's why I couldn't sleep in the first place. I just thought, here's my chance to get back at you, at all of you. So I laid him out on the table and put Shaker herbs on him like he'd been laid out for a ritual. That way, I thought Shakers would be blamed." He raised his eyes to Rose. "How'd you figure it was me?"

"May I speak with Seth privately for a moment?" Rose asked the sheriff.

Brock frowned.

"I'll tell you about it afterward, I promise."

"Yeah, OK, but just for a minute. I still figure Elsa's guilty. Maybe craziness just runs in the family."

"It was the fresh rosemary that led me to you," Rose said softly as she and Seth walked toward the middle of the village. "In the bouquet on Johann's chest, Gennie remembered finally that all the herbs and flowers were dried except the rosemary, as if someone had picked it especially. When we spoke the other day, you called me Rosie. That was one of your old nicknames for me, but there was another. I remembered that when we were together, I talked all the time about herbs, how to grow and use them. So after a while you started calling me Rosemary sometimes. You wanted me to remember that, didn't you?"

Seth nodded, his eyes cloudy. "I wanted you Shakers to be blamed for Johann, but I guess maybe I also wanted you to know I set it up. I wanted you to know you were being punished. I never expected you'd be the one to puzzle out the whole thing, not the sheriff. I figured you wouldn't let on what you knew, if it meant talking about you and me."

"Did you think I would let a Believer be arrested and say nothing, just to avoid discussing my own past?"

"OK, I was wrong to do what I did, but Rose, I didn't kill anyone, I swear. I swear I didn't."

Rose nodded slowly. "I think you could have, mind. If the bouquet hadn't disappeared from Johann's chest, I might still think you did do it. You had a lot to lose if Johann made good his threat to tell Peleg Webster he wasn't really your father. But there is someone with a great deal more to lose."

TWENTY-TWO

GENNIE PAUSED BEFORE THE BACK DOOR OF THE Carpenters' Shop. She really shouldn't talk to one of the men alone. But she couldn't just leave, either. It was partly her fault that Molly was dead. She had to follow whatever idea came to her. She reached for the doorknob, then withdrew her hand. She should at least go to the front door.

As she'd half turned to leave, the door jerked open, sending her tripping backwards. Sister Charity, her wide eyes nearly taking over her face, froze like one of the frightened jackrabbits Gennie often surprised in the herb fields. She shook herself and brushed past Gennie.

The door hung open. Gennie peeked inside. Everything seemed normal to her, so she ventured through the doorway. Albert worked in the far corner, his back to her. He wiped his hands on an old piece of dark-colored cloth, tossed it toward a pile of rags, and turned. A faint smile curved the edges of his mouth.

He glanced up and saw her, and his expression deadened. "How long you been standing there?" he asked in a mild voice.

"Just a moment or two," Gennie said. "I came to ask you a few things." She glanced back over her shoulder at the still-open door. "What happened to Charity? She looked upset."

Albert shrugged one shoulder and walked to his workbench. "Just a nervous type, I guess," he said. "She brought me some rags." He nodded vaguely in the direction of the back door. "No reason that should make her upset."

As if he were alone, he selected a wooden tool with a sharp edge that Gennie recognized as a planer and began to smooth a flat, rectangular piece of wood. His movements were fluid and precise. He ran strong, thin fingers along its edge to detect any rough spots.

Gennie thought she understood Charity's nervousness. Albert was so hard to talk to. She edged closer to the workbench. Albert didn't seem to notice. She took two more steps. His hand stopped. Without looking up, he said, "You shouldn't be here."

"Um, I know," Gennie said, relieved at the opportunity to speak. "But I wanted to ask you a few questions. You see, I noticed that your window upstairs looks right out on the Water House and, well, I wondered if you might have seen anything, anything at all, on the night of the fire. I mean, there might have been some noise, and you looked out, or surely you would have heard the fire, didn't you?"

"I sleep soundly," Albert said, glancing up briefly.

"Oh." Gennie took a deep breath. "You see, I was hoping you'd looked out your window. Because I did, and I saw someone running in front of the Water House while it burned. I think it was a woman because she was wearing a Dorothy cloak. It could have been Molly. Or it could have been the person who set the fire or maybe even Molly's killer."

Albert planed on, and Gennie grunted with impatience. Was this man unable to say more than three words at a time?

"Don't you see how important this is? If you saw anything, anything at all, then maybe we can figure out who killed Molly."

Albert smoothed his hand over his wood for the longest moments that Gennie had ever endured. This wasn't getting her anywhere.

"Nay," he said finally, "I slept until the fire bell rang. I saw nothing." His eyes darted toward Gennie and back again, almost shyly, to his task. "Sorry."

Gennie's shoulders slumped. "Me, too," she said.

She turned to the back door. Her eyes on the floor, she lifted her skirt and picked her way through sawdust and wood chips. The floor could use a good sweeping. She was about to mention this when she saw a bundle of old aprons and dishcloths, neatly wrapped with kitchen twine. The rags Charity had delivered. Gennie stopped so suddenly she dropped her skirt, stirred up some sawdust, and sneezed. One cloth peeked out from underneath the packet. The fabric looked like a fine dark blue wool, the kind the sisters used to make Dorothy cloaks.

"Albert?"

The carpenter swiveled on his bench and threw her an irritated glance.

"Are those the rags Charity brought?"

His eyes flicked to the pile of rags. He nodded.

Heedless now of the dust, Gennie rushed to the corner and fell to her knees. She shoved aside the bound-up rags and grabbed the blue fabric. Dirt and pulled threads marred the smooth, finely woven surface, and a large piece had been ripped out of its folds, but there was no mistaking the design. Gennie held the fabric to her nose. The fibers still held the acrid smell of smoke.

"I think I've found something really important," she said, while her shaking, eager fingers sought the neck lining of the cloak. "If Charity brought this, she must have been trying to get rid of it. Maybe she thought you'd cover it with paint and toss it out and she wouldn't have to figure out how to destroy it. Oh, here it is!" She smoothed out the inner neck lining. "I was right! M. F. for Molly Ferguson." She ran her index finger across the initials stitched into the fabric. "It's odd that Charity didn't rip this lining out before she brought the cloak over here."

Gennie felt Albert standing over her.

"Maybe she didn't have time," he said, his eyes on the fabric in her hands.

Gennie shrugged. "Must be." She gathered the soft folds in her arms and pushed to her feet. "I've got to get this to Grady. I mean Officer O'Neal."

"It isn't proper for a Shaker girl to talk to a policeman. I'll take it to him." Albert held out his hand.

Gennie wasn't about to let a chance to see—and maybe impress—Grady slip past her. "Oh, Albert, don't be silly. I've talked to policemen before. Besides, I'm remembering lots of things that I need to tell him. Like the fact that Charity wasn't in the kitchen after the worship service Sunday afternoon. I'll bet that's when she met Molly. Maybe that's when she killed her!" Albert folded his wiry arms across his chest.

"Oh, all right, you can come with me, if that will make it more proper." A corner of the cloak fell from Gennie's arms, and she bent down to recapture it. As she straightened, she again caught sight of the bundle of rags. A few loose rags still rested next to the bundle. One of them was a small piece of fine, dark blue wool, bearing distinct stains. Paint.

The rag that Albert had thrown aside when she entered had been dark blue. She remembered how it had landed, soft and heavy, on the edge of the pile. The truth hit her swiftly. Charity had not delivered the cloak. It was already there on the floor when Charity brought over her kitchen rags. It was Albert who hadn't yet had time to dispose of it or to remove the revealing initials from its lining. Maybe he'd just intended to rip it up and make it unrecognizable.

Albert stood between Gennie and the open back door.

Clutching the fabric with one arm and lifting her skirt with the other, she bolted for the front door. She was young and quick and halfway to the door already. She didn't look back, but she was sure that Albert hadn't expected her to move so fast.

A block of wood twisted her foot. She lost precious seconds regaining her balance, but she didn't fall. She was nearly there. She thought ahead with hope, saw herself burst through the door, run like a wild animal to the Trustees' Office. She dropped her skirt and reached for the doorknob. It turned, but the door didn't budge. She clutched the knob and threw her body against it. She hit solid wood.

She spun around to find Albert a few feet away, moving deliberately toward her, a small, wood-carving knife in his right hand. He paused before her and caressed the wooden handle with his thumb.

"I installed locks on these doors," he said. "Elder said to go ahead, you never know what mischief the world will make. Gives me more privacy, too. For some of the things I have to do."

"Now give me the cloak, Eugenie." His voice had a toneless quality, lacking even the warmth of anger. It chilled Gennie almost as much as the sharp blade pointing toward her. Her knees wanted to buckle. Through force of will, she kept them straight. She clutched the cloak, bunching it in front of her like a soft, thick shield.

Albert inched closer. "Hand it over," he said, with no show of impatience at having to repeat himself. "I'll get it one way or another. I'm capable of hurting pretty young girls. I think you know that."

The blade was now within inches of her. Instinctively, she stepped backward, and the doorknob hit the small of her back. He had her wedged in. If she tried to move sideways, he'd go for her at once.

"I won't wait much longer, little sister," Albert said, tilting his head to one side. "It's too bad, really.

Fredericks deserved what he got, but I'd rather not have to kill pretty young girls. I tried to let the other one live, I really did. I even bought her little baubles when she asked for them. But then she wanted money or she would tell the police what Fredericks had told her about me, what he found out about my past from his hobo buddies. She guessed that I killed him so he wouldn't give me away. She kept wanting more and more so she could leave here. I even hit her, but nothing stopped her demands. It wasn't safe to let her live any longer."

Gennie was astonished by his talkativeness. Maybe it was there all the time, hidden behind a fake reticence. Or maybe he had finally found a topic he enjoyed talking about. Gennie's bones felt chilled as though she had spent the night in the root cellar. But her mind clutched at this new knowledge about Albert. If she could use it to delay him, to save her life . . .

"So it was you I saw running from the Water House? You wore Molly's cloak so that if anyone saw you, they would think you were a sister. Molly was tall for a girl, so the cloak fit you."

Albert's face clouded. Gennie thought it might have been a mistake to call attention to his small stature.

"It was clever of you to think of using the cloak," she said quickly. "But why did you kill Johann in the first place?"

"I just said. He knew about me."

"We all knew you'd had some trouble with the law a long time ago. Why worry about that? You'd confessed it and been forgiven, hadn't you?"

Albert narrowed his eyes. She had pushed too hard. She grasped frantically for anything she could say, anything that would get him talking again.

"The herb bouquet," she said, trying to control the tremor in her voice, "what did that mean?"

Albert laughed without humor. "Nearly meant disaster, that's what. Somebody else's fool idea, like digging Fredericks up and moving him before I had a chance to bury him far away. Somebody tried to make it look like a Shaker did it. I couldn't afford that. Too close to home. They might start looking into my background."

Gennie nodded in what she hoped was a sympathetic manner. Albert ignored her.

"Good thing I was around when you found him, so I could sneak in and grab the herbs before the police got there. I figured they'd call you hysterical if you even remembered seeing them. Not that it did any good. That sheriff was so eager to blame a Shaker that he believed you anyway." Albert was very close to her now. "So now you know."

"Rose knows I'm here."

"I don't think so, little sister. You'd have said something long before now. Nay, I think we've got just enough time to do this right."

Gennie fought back the panic rising in her throat. She had to keep thinking, keep stalling him, until someone missed her. Rose would miss her, wouldn't she? If she screamed, would anyone even hear her? Or would Albert kill her instantly?

"You wanted to be a Believer," Gennie gasped in desperation. "How could you want to be a Believer and kill people?"

"I wanted to be a carpenter!" For the first time, Albert's voice took on some depth. "That's all I ever wanted."

"But you are a carpenter."

"A damn good one, too." He waved his free hand around the room, filled with his handiwork. But his eyes and his weapon still aimed at her. "Everyone says I'm gifted. But people keep interfering. It's the Depression, they said, nobody wants you, no matter how good you are. Sometimes someone would hire me and then they wouldn't pay me for all my beautiful work! That isn't fair, is it?"

"Nay, it's not fair."

His eyes flicked briefly around the shop, skimming over an unfinished table and an exquisite cabinet.

"They should not have done that to you," Gennie continued, trying to keep her voice steady, sympathetic.

"Damn right! Damn right they shouldn't have. They got what they deserved."

Now, Gennie thought, *now!* She lunged forward, pushing the bundle of thick wool directly into Albert's knife. Startled, he stumbled backwards. His grip loosened and the knife stuck in the fabric. Gennie sped around him in a wide arc. But Albert recovered quickly and sprinted across the floor toward her. He grabbed her skirt, pulling her off-balance. She twisted and fell on her back.

She still held the cloak, the knife stuck in the cloth. If Albert fell on her, the knife would go straight into her. With frantic, shaking fingers she felt for the wooden handle. She encountered the side of the blade first. She cried out as it ripped across her palm.

Gasping with pain, she located the handle and yanked the weapon out of the fabric. She tossed the cloak toward Albert, who batted it aside like a rubber ball. But the maneuver gained her a few seconds. She struggled to a standing position with her undamaged left hand and scrambled out of his reach.

"Stay away from me!" She held the knife in front of her, just as Albert had done earlier. Only her hand bled and shook badly. Albert smiled and strolled toward her, as though now he had all the time in the world. Gennie stumbled backwards. With a swift movement, Albert's sinewy hands grabbed her wrists. He squeezed her right wrist until her weakened fingers opened. The knife clattered to the floor. Albert ignored it and dragged her over to the rag pile as if she were light as a bundle of laundry.

Gennie filled her lungs and screamed for Rose. The

name was barely out of her mouth before it was replaced with a rag, tasting faintly of turpentine and stretched painfully across her teeth.

His bony face tight with concentration, Albert yanked her flailing arms behind her back and tied her wrists with a few loose rags. Pressing on her shoulders, he forced her down onto the rag pile, where he bound her ankles together and tied a final rag over her eyes.

He hoisted her up by the waist and threw her over one shoulder. She squirmed and tried to kick her bound legs, but his grip across her knees only tightened. The slight bounce in his step told her they were climbing the stairs.

They must have reached the second floor, because the climbing stopped. Gennie felt herself heaved backwards into what smelled like a wooden box. For a moment there was silence. Then Albert spoke again.

"Suppose you're wondering why I didn't just kill you downstairs," he said, so casually he might have been explaining why he had chosen to use a dark stain rather than a light one on a chest of drawers.

"Too messy. Blood. Hard to explain, if anyone comes looking for you before I get a chance to clean up. But don't worry. I'll take care of you later. You'll be so upset over Molly's death that you ran away. I'll fix it up. In the meantime, you'll be comfortable here. As long as there's air to breathe, that is. This was meant for Johann, by the way. You're small enough. Maybe you two can share it."

A soft, heavy cloth with a familiar smoky odor landed on top of Gennie. The cloak. As she strained to push it off her face with her chin, a lid dropped and shut out all sound and the sensations of light she had seen through the blindfold. The last sound she heard was the whack of a hammer pounding nails into the corners of what she now knew to be a pine coffin.

TWENTY-THREE

ROSE WATCHED SETH REJOIN THE CROWD OF BELIEVers gathering around Elsa and the police. It wasn't wise to do what she was about to do, but she had to be sure she was right. She'd never forgive herself if she handed an innocent person over to Brock.

The Carpenters' Shop was silent when she entered. At first she thought Albert must have joined the crowd. If so, she'd have to wait for her information.

She was about to leave when a soft creaking alerted her to someone's presence. Albert's thin legs slipped down the narrow wooden steps leading from his upstairs living quarters. On the bottom step, he paused and stared at her.

"The sheriff is arresting Elsa for murder," Rose said. "Are you going to let that happen?"

Albert shrugged. "Nothing I can do. If she's guilty, she should pay."

"Is she guilty?"

"Stands to reason, doesn't it? After Johann watched her practice that fake dancing of hers, he probably blackmailed her."

"Did Johann tell you that?"

"Told you, I barely spoke to the man."

"Then how did you know what Johann saw?"

Albert strolled to his workbench and slid onto his

stool, to all appearances relaxed. One hand draped loosely over the edge of the table.

"Were you keeping an eye on Johann, watching his movements and waiting for the right moment to dispose of him? Johann tried to blackmail you, too, didn't he? For something much worse than dancing."

Albert snorted. "That's nonsense."

"I made a telephone call to Massachusetts, to the Hancock Society. I should have thought to make the call earlier, as soon as I remembered that you'd spent time in prison. But I didn't at first put that together with two other facts about you—your skill in making Shaker furniture and your Eastern accent."

Albert tilted his head and regarded her with one, too-bright eye, like a sparrow assessing danger in the rustling undergrowth.

"The eldress at the Hancock Society told me that the sudden departure of their carpenter, Bert Findlay, coincided with a tragic occurrence in a nearby village. The richest man in town—and also the most miserly—was found stabbed to death in his home. Near his body was an exquisite desk of Shaker design, quite new. The eldress said that she had suspected for some time that Brother Bert was selling some of the furniture he made and pocketing the money. She had been planning to confront him about it when he disappeared."

Albert's thumb began to rub the edge of the work-table.

"Bert Findlay was a short, wiry man. He matched your description perfectly."

"Lots of men look like me."

"But not many who are skilled in Shaker carpentry."

Albert raised one shoulder in a tiny shrug. "I learn fast."

"You killed Johann and Molly. You also burned down the barn to throw suspicion on the townspeople and the Water House to dispose of Molly's body, didn't you?"

Slow seconds passed. Rose was acutely aware of the ticking of a clock, the scraping sound as the carpenter dragged a length of wood toward himself, her own thudding heart.

"You'd do better to tell me. The Society will help you. We'll find you a lawyer, a good one. You know we abhor the death penalty; we'll fight any effort to impose it on you."

As Albert's thin lips curled into a snarl, the door behind Rose crashed open and slammed against the wall. She spun around to see Sheriff Brock and Grady burst into the room, their guns drawn. Seth slid in behind them.

"Where's Gennie? What have you done with her?" Grady shouted.

"Gennie? What do you mean? What are you saying?" Rose searched the men's faces, looking for the answer she was afraid to hear.

Seth edged forward. "You talked like you knew who the killer was," he said softly to Rose, "and then I saw you go off toward the Carpenters' Shop. So I told the sheriff. Charity was there, and she said she brought Albert some rags and saw a Shaker woman's cloak on the floor here. She also said that Gennie was at the door when she left."

"You're all crazy," Albert said. "The girl just wanted to ask if I'd seen the fire, and she left right away."

"Don't believe him. This man's real name is Bert Findlay," Rose called over her shoulder as she dropped to her knees before Albert's rags. She rooted frantically through the disheveled pile, tossing aside the frayed remains of summer dresses and dish towels as she searched for the fine, dark wool of a Shaker Dorothy cloak.

"I spoke with the eldress at the Hancock Society and found out he's wanted for murder in Massachusetts."

"Oh yeah?" Sheriff Brock said. "Maybe we'll be using those handcuffs after all—Findlay, is it?"

Rose stared at one bit of cloth, a scrap of light blue-and-white-striped cotton. It was worn and shredded and spotted with fresh red splotches. She grabbed a handful of rags. Two others clearly were splattered with blood, still tacky to the touch.

"Explain this." Rose swiveled on her knees toward Albert. "This is blood, isn't it? Where did it come from?"

Brock grabbed the cloth from her hands and tossed them to Grady. "Well, Findlay?"

"I cut my hand," Albert said evenly. "Happens a lot in my work. Used the rag to stop the bleeding."

"You cut your hand over here, where you have no tools, and then dripped blood on all these other rags?" Rose faced Albert and thrust a stained cloth under his nose.

"And while you're at it," Grady said, "explain this." He bent over a small chest next to the workbench. One drawer hung open. In his hand, Grady held an open envelope from which a stack of green bills poked out.

Too late, Rose realized that she stood between Albert and the police. Grady and Brock surged forward, but not quickly enough. Albert's hand flew to the worktable and grabbed his wood-carving knife. He held it to Rose's neck, while the strong fingers of his left hand wrenched her arm behind her back.

"Stop where you are," Albert warned, "or the knife goes in where it's aimed. I've got nothing to lose. It'll take more than Shaker lawyers to keep them from killing me this time."

Albert threw a startled glance up the narrow staircase. Rose heard it, too, a pounding noise, just upstairs. For a moment, Albert's grip relaxed. Rose wrenched free of his grip and, with all her strength, shoved him backwards, directly into the path of an unfinished rocking chair. He and the chair flipped backwards and crashed. No sooner had he hit the floor than Brock and Grady jerked him upright and forced his wrists into handcuffs behind his back.

Rose flew up the stairs toward the source of the pounding. In the carpenter's retiring room, she found a plain pine coffin. Grady appeared at her shoulder. The pounding began again, and it came from inside the coffin.

"It's Gennie, it's got to be!" Grady cried. He spun around and located a hammer, tossed on top of Albert's bed. He wrenched up the nails securing the coffin lid. Together, he and Rose heaved it up and slid it to the floor. Gennie squirmed inside.

"Smart girl!" Grady lifted Gennie carefully to a sitting position, eased off the gag and blindfold. With a flick of his pocketknife, he slashed through the rags binding her hands. Gennie sobbed hoarsely and threw her arms around his neck. He lifted her tenderly and held her.

Rose averted her eyes. She had broken her own pledge of nonviolence today. She did not feel capable of judging Gennie, who had not yet taken the same vows. And, it seemed, might never do so. Nevertheless, Rose found herself smiling.

TWENTY-FOUR

A HALLOWEEN WIND PIERCED THE CORNERS OF ROSE'S bonnet despite the added protection of her cloak hood. She and Gennie walked between the lightly frosted rows of the herb fields, their feet crunching in unison.

"Are you too cold?" Rose asked. "Shall we go back?"

Gennie shook her head and gazed across the herb fields.

"I love these fields." She turned to Rose. "And I love all of you. You know that, don't you?"

"Yea."

They walked on in silence for a time, catching their capes when they flew open and watching the ground for slippery patches.

Gennie broke the silence first. "Rose?" she asked tentatively.

"You asked me to walk with you this morning because you had something to tell me?"

"How did you know?"

Rose flashed a smile. "It wasn't difficult. Besides, according to Grady O'Neal, I've proved myself to be a fair detective."

"Well, that's part of what I wanted to talk about. About some of the things I still don't understand about what happened, and . . . about Grady."

"You're leaving, aren't you, Gennie?" Rose tried to keep the sorrow out of her voice.

"Grady asked me if we could see each other. He said to tell you he'd treat me with respect. He wants us to think about getting married."

"And what did you tell him?"

"I said I'm only seventeen. I said I wouldn't marry anyone until I'm at least nineteen."

Rose saw with a touch of pride that Gennie held her chin high. Unlike the tragic Molly, Gennie would not be pressured.

"What was his response?"

"He said that was smart. And he said that . . . that I could stay with his sister . . . after I leave. Isn't that funny, Rose? Remember the girl in the red dress who stopped in the police station to see Grady? I thought she was his girlfriend, but she's his sister, Emily! He's been keeping a close eye on her because she's so pretty, and Johann tried to . . . well, you know, get too friendly with her, and Grady was afraid she'd be suspected of having something to do with his getting killed.

"Grady said that she works in a flower shop in town, and she could try to get me a job there. Maybe I could talk them into using herb flowers. Then I wouldn't have to leave everything so . . . so completely."

Gennie chattered happily and Rose let her. She saw they were approaching the old cemetery, one of Molly's favorite hideaways. To her left, across the village's central pathway, she could just see the burned-out Water House, and the empty Carpenters' Shop, boards nailed across the smashed door. There was no one left to fix it. Maybe it was for the best, Gennie's leaving. The best for Gennie, anyway, not for the Society. And not for Rose. Maybe Gennie would decide not to marry after all. Maybe she would come back. It had happened before.

"I never thought that Charity would leave," Gennie was saying.

"What? Ah, Charity. Yea, she has decided to leave, at least for a time."

"But why? She didn't hurt anyone, did she? She didn't even trip someone over a rocking chair, like you did." Gennie giggled, something Rose hadn't heard her do for some time. For the giggle, she forgave Gennie's making light of violence.

"Anyway," Gennie continued, "I'm glad that Wilhelm's stopped trying to make Elsa into Mother or even eldress."

Rose shook her head sadly. "Wilhelm has been wounded in spirit."

"You feel sorry for him? After the way he treated you? He wanted to send you away!"

"Wilhelm was betrayed. Worse yet, he betrayed himself. He is not a man who can easily live with that knowledge. And as it turns out, he'd been struggling with suspicion for some time. The night he found you in the cemetery, he had followed Elsa out to the herb fields. Elsa practiced her dancing and suddenly began to speak in tongues. Then she stopped and started again, as if perfecting her performance. Wilhelm wanted her behavior to be evidence of divine spirit, but he was haunted by the fear that she had more in mind than he'd bargained for."

"At least Charity's much better off," Gennie said. "She can run the kitchen just as she wishes. So why would she want to leave?"

"She did abandon the kitchen after the public worship service," Rose said.

"I know," Gennie said. "I found the kitchen empty when I was searching for Molly."

"She lost her nerve, ran to hide in her retiring room. She must be able to face such adversity if she is to be a Believer. But it isn't only that. Charity confessed to me what has been troubling her. Since she is leaving, we agreed that the Society need not know."

"So you can't tell me what happened?"

Rose shook her head.

"Not even if I try to guess?"

"Gennie!" Rose scolded, and laughed at the same time. But she said nothing more about Charity. Poor Charity, in love for the first time with Johann Fredericks, who used her for his pleasure and left her with a guilt so profound that it was killing her a moment at a time. She accepted full responsibility for her behavior, she had told Rose. She had broken her vows. She could not stay. Rose sighed. Surely Mother Ann had been right. Celibacy was truly the most blessed way of life.

She felt Gennie's eyes flash to her face as though reading her thoughts.

"Um, Rose?" Gennie said.

"Hm?"

"Would you explain something to me sometime soon, before I leave?"

"If I can. What is it?"

Gennie bit her lip. "Would you tell me exactly what it means not to be chaste?"